CW00859447

Micahs Ember

By Nicola C. Matthews

Micah's Ember

Published by

Taboo Tales

A division of X-Isle United Press

The characters and events portrayed in this book are fictitious. Any similarity to real persons, living or dead, or to any other written publication is coincidental and not intended by the author.

Cover art and interior graphics by

Bloody Feather Graphix Team

Micah's Ember

For Micah – one of the coolest guys I've met. Wishing you a long and prosperous career. May all your dreams come true.

Micah's Ember

Chapter 1

Ember grunted as the email alerts on her cell phone began going off one after the other. She looked down, watching as the silenced device stealthily shook its way across the bathroom counter. She wondered for perhaps the hundredth time why in hell she had agreed to have her work emails synced to her phone. All it meant was she went from being a salaried employee working for ten hours a month for free to being on-call twenty-four hours a day, seven days a week.

She had spent the last eight years of her life trying to climb up what constituted as the 'corporate ladder' in the multi-million dollar tech company she had been working for ever since she had graduated from college. She had spent all that time working her ass off doing twice the work for one-third the pay a man would have received for doing the same job. Despite her boss telling her four times in as many years she was receiving a raise, she was actually making *less* money now than she was when she first started. She still hadn't figured out how that was even possible.

She frowned at her reflection in the mirror. Just the thought of all the hoops she was forced to jump through on a daily basis made her blood boil. While she knew she had been passed over for promotions time and again because she was

Micah's Ember

female, she also knew there was jack-shit she could do about it.

The company was owned by a man, every vice president in the company was a man, and after so many years of clawing her way up that joke of a corporate ladder, she knew she should just be thankful they hadn't hired a *man* to come in and take over the project management position she currently held. Never mind she had not only created the management process their company had adopted, but she also had been single-handedly managing all their projects since the company decided to implement the process.

She sighed, picking up her phone in one hand as she tried to apply mascara with the other one. Her bright blue eyes darted back and forth between the screen on her phone and her own reflection, praying she didn't accidentally stab herself in the eye. At least if that happened she might actually get a vacation day for once.

She looked at her email alerts, seeing more than two dozen new emails sitting in her corporate inbox. She forced herself to click out of it. She would be in her office in less than two hours. No matter what was in the email, there wasn't much she could do until she was logged into the company project management system. Until then, her audio-visual team would just have to wait until she finally made it to her desk.

Ember tossed the phone to the side, giving it a sideways glance as a new Snapagram message alert popped up in her alerts menu. Curious, she capped her tube of mascara and opened the app, wondering if maybe she had finally broken the five-hundred mark on her followers. She had been posting under a fake name for the better part of two years now, mostly ridiculous memes she had

Micah's Ember

found online, but she also posted the occasional burlesque-type selfies as well.

She had a love of metal and rock music, so most of the accounts she followed were band accounts and their individual members. Every now and again one of the band accounts or members would start to follow her, oftentimes making her giddy with happiness. Her regular job was so damn boring and stressful, it was always a treat for her when she was able to connect with artists. She dabbled in graphic artwork and photography, so the musicians, the music, the tattoos, the body modifications and everything else which went along with the scene greatly intrigued her.

She eyed the little comment alert, wondering who could possibly be looking at her profile this early in the morning. Her thumb hovered over the tiny icon before pressing it, her phone making a cute swooping noise as it pulled up the latest message.

@theEternalEmber Thanks for all the likes!

She looked at the name attached to the comment, recognizing it immediately. Her small, pink mouth popped open as more notifications came in on Snapagram – three "likes" on various photos of her, and a new notification that Micah Vaughn, the drummer of the alternative metal band *Tempered Souls*, was now following her account.

She paused, smiling like a dumbass. She didn't know why it excited her so much to hang out with musicians. It was just a painful reminder of how her music journalism career had somehow morphed into her getting a business degree and working herself to death to make some other fucker rich. Despite her dreams not panning out quite like she had hoped, she still had a fierce love

Micah's Ember

of music, concerts, and anything related to the music industry and the musicians behind it.

@TSMicah You're welcome! I've been stalking you guys for a few months now.

She hit the send button on the comment and tossed her phone to the side as she squirted hair gel into her hands, quickly rubbing it into the roots of her strawberry blonde hair before picking up her hair dryer. She ignored her phone when it started vibrating a few seconds later, thinking it was just more work related emails.

She worked the dryer through her short hair, pausing to rub more styling gel into the roots before she finished drying it. She washed her hands, glancing at her phone as it let out another long buzz. Wondering who could possibly be sending her emails at five in the morning, she picked it up, surprised to see Micah had sent her another message.

@theEternalEmber That's awesome!

Ember paused for a few seconds, that silly smile on her face again. She debated on responding, figuring he wouldn't keep messaging her. She had had a few bands chat with her through social media from time to time, but it was usually nothing more than a few quick words, thanks for being a fan, check out our new album, and that was it.

She shrugged. Why not? The most he could do was ignore her.

@TSMicah I was a bit upset when I saw your tour dates for the rest of the year ☹

She went to set the phone down again, only to have it immediately begin to buzz as a new alert came through. She swiped the screen open, once again surprised to see Micah had answered her.

@theEternalEmber Why is that?

Micah's Ember

@TSMicah You guys aren't coming anywhere near me.

She quickly opened up their profile, double-checking their tour dates. Yes, the closest they were going to be in the next few months was an entire day's worth of travel from Louisiana. There was no way she could make that even if she were able to get a day off from work.

@theEternalEmber Sorry to hear. Maybe next time? I would love to meet you.

Ember stared at her phone, somehow managing to frown and smile at the same time.

@TSMicah Aww, I'd love to meet you, too! Just remember us metal-head rednecks need love too

@theEternalEmber LOL I'll keep that in mind. How long have you been a fan?

She thought back, not really sure how she had come across the band or when. She was bad about watching music videos and just letting them play in the background as she worked, the videos playing an oddball assortment of various bands in the same genres. She had found so many of her new favorite bands this way, but she honestly had no idea how she had come across *Tempered Souls*. She had purposely clicked on the link they had posted on their Snapagram profile to their last music video, so she knew she must have already had them on her friends list prior to even listening to them.

@TSMicah About six months I think?

@theEternalEmber That's great! Maybe we'll catch you next tour.

She smiled, trying to think of a witty comment that didn't come off as being too snarky.

@TSMicha That would be great. Hope you don't mind eccentric people. I can get a bit crazy at times.

@theEternalEmber Crazy is cool.

Micah's Ember

@TSMicah Good. Most people don't get my weird sense of humor.

@theEternalEmber Same here.

She smiled again. She couldn't believe she was having this conversation with the drummer of one of her new fave bands. She had had bands reply to her comments on their posts, but never had she had an actual conversation with any of them.

@TSMicah Do you laugh at weird things that most people don't really get? And they look at you like you're nuts?

@theEternalEmber YES!! All the time.

@TSMicah LOL me too.

She glanced at the time on her phone, cursing silently as she realized she had spent the last half-hour chatting with him.

@TSMicah Fuck! I'm going to be late for work. It was nice chatting with you. Hit me up anytime.

@theEternalEmber Sure thing. Have a good day.

Ember smiled as she struggled to get her small tits into her bra, tossing her phone into her purse as she strolled past the bar which separated her small living room from her kitchen. She had a lot of paperwork to do for her side business, and she was now officially running late. She decided it didn't matter. For the first time in months she felt like a regular person with a real, interesting life which someone else was willing to peek into, if only for a moment.

Sighing, she dug out a pair of charcoal dress pants and slipped them on her long legs, pairing it with a nice sweater which did little to emphasize her round hips and slightly tapered waist.

She once again wished she could afford to stay home and create book covers and photographs like she had always dreamed of doing. She wished she had more willpower to stay away from the late-

Micah's Ember

night chocolate binges which kept the extra fifteen pounds sitting around her thighs and upper arms. She wished she could afford a private trainer to put her sagging ass back where it had been twenty years ago. But perhaps more than anything, she wished she had someone in her life who would actually listen to what she had to say, and not tell her he didn't care how stressed she was at work.

That was the problem with dreams, though. No matter how hard and fast she chased them, they always seemed to slip further and further away just as she reached out to grasp them.

Micah's Ember

Chapter 2

I don't understand how this keeps happening. This makes four times this month invoices have been misplaced.

Ember stared at the email on her computer screen, trying not to grind her teeth together. She wasn't sure which she wanted to do more, punch her fist through the monitor or tell her jackass of a boss she couldn't be held responsible for what he did with his shit once she handed it over to him.

"Every motherfucking time," she hissed under her breath, slamming down the small stack of invoices she had been holding in her hand. She slid her chair over to the filing cabinet, pulling out the duplicate copy of the invoice her boss had misplaced, once again, for the fourth or fifth time this month.

She walked out of her small corner cubicle and around to the back of the large, open room which housed the special projects and sales division of the company. She passed by several of her coworkers, busy chatting or staring at their cell phones, and she once again felt her blood boil as she remembered her boss telling her explicitly she was not allowed to have her cell phone out of her desk drawer at all during regular work hours. It appeared, however, as she rounded the corner of her boss' cubicle to see him texting on his own

Micah's Ember

phone, that the rule only applied to certain people in the company.

"Here's a copy of the invoice," she said in a flat monotone, forcing herself to smile as her boss looked up from his phone.

"Where was it?" he asked as he went back to texting, not even bothering to try to hide the fact he had been on the damn thing.

"This is a duplicate. I gave you the original two weeks ago. I have no idea what you did with it after that, Tanner."

He nodded, reaching out his hand without looking up from his phone. She resisted the urge to smack him upside his befuddled head with the invoice and payment sheet. Instead, she slipped the small stack of papers into his outstretched hand, turning sharply on her heel to go back to her own cubicle.

"Have you moved Friday's meetings to Thursday yet?" Tanner asked, causing her to pause.

"No, why would I reschedule the conference calls?"

"Aren't you going to be coming in late on Friday?"

She bit her tongue, forcing herself to not hiss as she replied, "Yes."

"Then you need to reschedule them. Part of project management is keeping up with what is going on with all the projects we currently have open on the books. That means these weekly meetings cannot be missed."

Holy. *Shit*. Was he for real?

She dug her nails into her hand, reminding herself she had to have this job if she expected to be able to keep her mortgage payments current. The only good thing about being single was the fact she only had to cook and clean for one person.

Micah's Ember

Paying the bills, however, was a weekly struggle, especially considering she was getting paid less than a fourth of what she was actually worth.

Last fucking time I checked, the word "manager" wasn't anywhere in my damn job description, you fucking bastard, she thought to herself.

"Yes sir, I'll get everything changed for Thursday."

"Good, be sure to resend out the invites, copy me."

Fucking prick, not my fault you are either too fucking lazy or stupid to know how to do my job, and you probably making three times what I do.

"Yes, sir," she said instead as she turned back around, quickly walking to her own cubicle before she told the fucker off and ended up homeless by the end of the month.

***

"Un-fucking-believable," Nicci said as Ember recounted that morning's story. "I swear to all that is holy, I am so fucking fed up with this company and all the shit that goes on."

Ember nodded, sipping her cup of coffee. She really needed a Margarita right about now, but she didn't want to give them any reason to write her up or fire her. She knew her boss would lose his shit if something happened to her. Even though he didn't like to admit it, he knew she was the one who was pretty much running the entire department at this point.

His dementia was getting so bad he was literally forgetting to go to meetings and misplacing documents on a daily basis. She had gone from just heading up the special projects to being his stand-in assistant, constantly reminding him of

Micah's Ember

things he needed to do. It had gotten so bad, in fact, that for the last four years everyone else in the department came to her with their work-related problems rather than him. She usually got the problem resolved within a day. With Tanner, it could be months later and he still would not have a resolution for the simplest of problems.

"I don't get it, Nicci," she said as she took off her glasses and rubbed the bridge of her nose. "I've worked my ass off for years, I have everyone on both my AV and networking team asking our VP to promote me to special projects manager and hire me an assistant to take some of this other crap off my hands, and yet here I am, basically getting fucked over, and not in a good way."

"What did they say?"

"About what?" she asked, momentarily confused.

"And you think Tanner's memory is bad?" Nicci joked, tossing a French fry at her friend's head.

Ember laughed. "Oh, you mean about the promotion?" She snorted. "Tanner's answer is always, 'Ember is already doing that, we don't need to hire anyone else.' So basically they won't promote me and give me a fucking pay raise because I've already been doing this job, without complaint, for four years now." She tossed her napkin onto the table and sat back in her chair, crossing her arms beneath her small breasts.

"Hmm, then I see where the problem is."

"What's that," she asked, one perfectly plucked reddish-blonde eyebrow raised in question.

"You don't have a dick."

She snorted again. "Yeah I do, his name is Tanner."

Micah's Ember

They both started laughing, the other guests in the restaurant looking at them as they guffawed for five minutes straight.

"But seriously, Em, you know they walk all over you because you're a woman."

"Mmm hmm," she murmured as she sipped her coffee, grimacing as the lukewarm brew hit her tongue. "Yeah, I know. I'd be getting paid six figures to do this shit if I were male. How is it we've come so far as women and yet still be so far down the damn proverbial totem pole?"

Nicci shrugged. "Hell if I know, girl. If I could figure that shit out I'd be rich by now, and then I wouldn't have to worry about a man, or a job, or any damn thing else other than making sure I had plenty of cute asses to stare at all day."

Ember giggled before groaning aloud as her phone let out a tiny chirp, alerting her to another email.

"Regretting that shit now?" Nicci asked as she watched Ember swipe her thumb across her smartphone.

"Hell yeah," she said, relieved to see it was another alert coming through on her Snapagram account.

She loaded the app, surprised to see another message from Micah.

You still at work?

Just getting in from lunch actually. What's up?

Oh, didn't mean to bother you. Chat you later maybe?

Sure, she replied. *Hit me up on Skipper?*

Okay. Same screen name?

You know it ☺

Ember set her phone down, stopping as she saw the questioning look on Nicci's face. "What?"

"Why are you suddenly smiling like the cat that ate the canary?"

Micah's Ember

"What the hell are you talking about?" Ember asked as she gathered up her purse and car keys, ready to get this day over with before she blew a gasket.

"That smile. Last time I saw you smile like that was when the mail guy asked you out." She paused, gasping. "Oh my fucking gawd, you ho-bag you. You're dating someone, aren't you? And you didn't bother to tell me? What the hell?"

Ember laughed as they walked back to her car. "I'm not dating anyone. If I were, you'd be the first to know."

"Uh, huh, sure you're not."

"I'm not, Nicci. Really. I don't have time to date anyone. And who the hell wants a washed-up cougar staring down the barrel of her fortieth birthday anyway? The only 'action' my thighs are getting these days is when they rub together as I chase down the garbage truck on trash day."

Her friend let out a loud giggle as they climbed into her sedan. "Come on, I know your work emails didn't cause you to have a smile like that on your face. So what gives? You finally get a paying client wanting headshots who happens to also be built like a brick shit-house?"

Ember almost choked on the swallow of soda she had gulped down as they exited on the intestate, causing her to swerve into on-coming traffic as horns blared. She coughed a few times before bursting into laughter.

"I wish, you horn-dog. No, nothing like that. I just had the drummer of one of my new favorite bands strike up a conversation with me on Snapagram this morning. He messaged me again is all." She shrugged. "I guess it's just nice to have someone to talk to about music from a non-fangirl point of view. No offense," she added quickly.

Micah's Ember

Nicci grinned at her. "None taken. So is this guy cute?"

"What difference does that make?"

"Uh, huh, he's a total hottie, isn't he?"

"It doesn't matter, Nicci. He's nice and I really like the band's sound and-" She shrugged again, at a loss for words.

"Oh yeah, definitely a hottie then."

Ember started laughing again. "Okay, *yes*, if you must know, he's cute as fuck. Happy now?"

Nicci snorted. "And you call me the horn-dog, you damn old perv."

"Watch who you are calling a perve. Last time I checked, you had this whole elaborate plan to kidnap the singer of *Profane Remains*. And he's like, what, twenty-five?"

"He's in his thirties, thank you very much. You're thinking of that time I had planned to kidnap Andy Savage. He was barely in his twenties when he was embraced."

The two of them grinned at each other as her white car barreled down the interstate, whisking them both back to their respective jobs and all the headaches which came with them.

Micah's Ember

Chapter 3

What are you up to?

Ember looked at the new message on her Skipper account, smiling as she sipped her glass of wine.

Just got out of the shower, relaxing with a glass of wine.

Rough day?

She almost snorted.

You have no idea lol she replied as she flipped through her Snapagram feed. Suddenly a photo caught her eye, one of the very person she was currently chatting with, a candid selfie of him sprawled out on his bed, sans shirt.

Holy fuck, she thought to herself as she immediately hit the "like" button on the photo.

Who took the pic?

Which one?

She wasn't sure if she should laugh or start fanning herself.

That last one on Snapagram, you on the bed.

She waited impatiently for his reply as she scrolled through his timeline feed, watching the short one minute videos of him during various practice sessions. He was not the typical-looking metal-head musician, and certainly not someone who fit her usual 'type.' She expected her metal heads to be more tattoos than skin, more piercings

Micah's Ember

than flesh, sporting eyeliner and ripped fishnets. Basically, anyone who looked like a Marilyn Manson fangirl reject.

Micah, however, looked like he belonged in a boy-band more than an alternative metal band. His hair was cut short, and unless he was hiding some serious piercings below the waist, his ears and a small, single nose piercing were the only extra holes she could see. He was broad-shouldered with a tapered waist, a square jawline and full lips which made her both jealous and aroused at the same time. His aquamarine eyes had a sleepy look to them, an altogether All-American boy-next-door vibe which both intrigued her and sent her senses reeling in equal amounts.

I did

She stared at his reply, debating on whether or not she should ask him what was really on her mind.

Do you think I look hot in that pic?

Ember choked on the sip of wine she had just taken, staring open-mouthed at her phone. She had to re-read the question, not sure the liquor induced haze in her brain had processed the words correctly.

She paused before answering. *I think you are cute as fuck.*

LOL that means hot, right?

She tossed back the rest of her red wine, not really sure where this was going. Maybe he was just making conversation.

In your case, hell yes ☺

She got up to pour herself another glass of wine, struggling to get the cork out of the bottle. As she picked up her glass, a photo came through her messenger, a photo of a very naked and very damn fine-looking male ass.

Micah's Ember

"Holy fuck me running!" she hissed, resisting the urge to lick her phone. "I know what photo I'm using as my new wallpaper on my desktop," she whispered, her eyes wide as they roamed over every inch of his scrumptious derriere.

The front looks even better ;)

She gulped.

I bet it does she replied.

Don't you wanna see?

She felt her face flush only to have it take a complete nose-dive to her groin, the bolt of electric arousal hitting her so hard she nearly groaned.

"How the fuck am I supposed to answer that?" she wondered aloud, wanting to see but at the same time feeling like the biggest damn perv on the planet. This kid was literally half her age.

Hell yeah, but I think that maybe taking things a bit too far, don't you?

She picked up her glass of wine and headed back to her bedroom, settling back among the plush red and black pillows.

Why do you say that?

She sipped her wine, using one thumb to type in her answer.

I'm practically old enough to be your mum. Doesn't that creep you out?

I don't mind if you don't ;)

She groaned as she tossed her phone to the side, opting to pull out her tablet so she wouldn't have to keep erasing half of what she typed. She really disliked using the tiny screen-generated keyboard on her phone. Plus the damn thing kept trying to auto-correct half of what she typed which was why it took her so long to reply to a message.

She logged into her Skipper account just in time to see an incoming call from Micah. Her heart leapt into her throat. Should she answer it?

Micah's Ember

Why the hell not? she thought to herself. She figured the worst that could happen was her perverted sense of humor would scare him off, possibly for good. That, or her complete lack of makeup and sagging neckline. Fuck, it sucked getting old. Her mind kept thinking it was twenty until her eyes looked down. It always made her wonder what the fuck had happened. She wasn't sure at what point her ass started sagging but she most definitely was *not* happy about it.

She clicked on the green *accept* button, holding her tablet up a bit so he wouldn't get a full screen of her braless cleavage hanging out of her tank top. She couldn't help but smile as she saw him on the screen, propped up in his bed just as she currently was. His photos just didn't do him justice.

"Hey," she said, feeling like a complete idiot as she waved at her tablet.

He smiled, waving back. "Hey yourself."

"So what are you doing?" she asked after a brief second-long silence, taking another sip of wine as she eyed him over the rim of her glass.

His smile broadened. "Hitting on an older woman. And I see I was right."

She raised an eyebrow. "Oh really, what were you right about?"

"That you're just as beautiful in person."

She burst into laughter, the sound musical as it echoed off the walls of her bedroom. "My, don't you have a set on you."

He grinned back at her. "Is that a yes then?"

"For what?" she asked, a lop-sided grin on her face.

"I asked if you wanted to see it."

She flushed, once again feeling the heat rush to her center as she remembered the photo he had sent of his perfect little ass.

Micah's Ember

"Oh sweetie, this isn't a case of *I'll show you mine if you show me yours* is it?"

He shrugged. "Not unless you want to show me yours."

"Don't you think you should at least offer me a drink before you start stripping?"

"You already have a drink," he pointed out as he nodded at the glass of Merlot in her hand. He leaned over a tiny bit as he picked up the beer sitting beside him on the nightstand, raising it in a silent toast to her. "And I've got mine."

"So does this mean we're having our first date then?"

"Mmm, I always wanted to date an older woman."

She tried not to snort. Damn, this kid certain had balls, she would give him that much.

"I'm not sure you would know what to do with an older woman."

He stuck his tongue out, wagging it up and down as if he were licking an invisible ice-cream cone. It was so damn cute, she started giggling.

"Exactly how much have you had to drink? And are you even legal to buy beer?"

He laughed with her. "Yeah, I'm twenty-two. And this is my first one." He eyed her as she sipped her wine.

"What about you? How many glasses does that make?"

"Mmm, just my second. And you should be careful about sticking your tongue out like that, especially when you're on stage."

"Why's that?"

"Because some cougar might snatch your cute ass off the stage and shove her tongue down your throat. It may or may not be me, I'm just sayin'"

He raised an eyebrow, a slow grin spreading across his face. "Is that a promise?"

Micah's Ember

"More like a threat."

"Nope, too late, no take backs. Now you've got to kiss me when we meet."

I'd like to do a hell of a lot more than just kiss you, she thought to herself.

"So what are you up to tonight? It's Friday, shouldn't you be out with friends or something?"

"I could ask you the same thing."

"That's an easy one," she said with a laugh. "My idea of a night out is spending it curled up with a good book, or a good movie."

"Not much for partying?"

She shook her head as she adjusted her position in the bed. "No, not since my twenties. I spend so much time trapped inside a cubicle at work, spending time at home is actually a treat for me. What about you?"

"What about me?"

She gave him a crooked grin. "Stop being coy. Why aren't you out enjoying your youth, hanging out with friends or playing a show?"

He shrugged. "We're going on tour in a few months, we've been in the studio for the last eight months straight laying down new tracks. Knowing I'm about to spend the next four months of my life crammed into a tiny van with four other guys makes me want to hunker down and enjoy my own bed while I have the chance."

She nodded in agreement. "I can understand that. So you're just relaxing at home?"

"Mmm hmm," he replied as he took another sip of his beer. "So what do you do? You said you spend all day in a cubicle."

She groaned. "Ugh, I work for a technology reseller. I don't have an official title, I'm just considered 'sales support.' But if you want to get down to the nut-cutting, technically I'm the special projects manager for the company."

Micah's Ember

"What does that mean, 'special projects'?"

"Well, we don't just sell technology equipment, we also do audio-visual room design and networking design as well as install the products we sell. It's my job to track all the equipment which gets ordered, make sure my territory project managers and sales team know when there are problems, make sure my subcontractors get purchase orders issued as well as get paid for the work-" she stopped, realizing she was babbling. "Sorry, I keep forgetting what I do isn't easily described and if you don't work for the company it's nearly impossible to wrap your head around." She paused before adding, "Let's just say I do *a lot* of paperwork."

"No, it's fine. It actually sounds like you have a really difficult job."

She nodded as she took another swallow of wine. "That's putting it mildly."

"Stressful I bet."

She lifted her glass. "Yep, hence the liquid courage after five every day," she said with a grin.

"Damn, what the hell did you study in school?"

"Business management."

"Do you mind me asking what you make?"

"Mostly inappropriate comments and smart-ass retorts."

He laughed. "That bad huh?"

"Let's just say the only thing I'm managing at that job is my temper, and these days I'm not really doing a very good job of it. I should get a bonus check for every day I go without smacking the shit out of one of my coworkers."

They both laughed, sitting in comfortable silence for a few minutes. "Did you always want to study business?"

Micah's Ember

She grimaced. "Hell no. I wanted to study music journalism, or photography, but that shit doesn't pay the bills. And unfortunately, I live in a tiny little town where jobs are very hard to come by, especially if you don't have a dick and don't know someone who can pull some strings to get your foot in the door."

He nodded. "I think that's the way it is everywhere. But I'm glad to hear you don't have a dick. That might make things awkward."

She giggled. "So you're not secretly hiding a vagina in your pants, right?"

He raised his eyebrow. "That reminds me, I never showed you the front."

"Oh, stop it now," she said a bit breathlessly, her face flushing.

"Damn, I made you blush. I can't believe it." He paused for a second, not sure he should ask but still wanting to know. "What are you wearing?"

"You want to see what I'm wearing?" she asked as she lowered her voice, looking at him through her lashes.

He nodded his head, his eyes shining brightly in the dim light of his bedroom.

"Hold on," she said as she took her selfie-stick and attached it to her tablet using the extension she had rigged. She extended the handle, the tablet rising a good foot above her, giving Micah a view of her sitting in her bed.

His eyes roamed over her tank-top and pajama-shorts as she smiled at him, wondering what on earth he could possibly find even remotely attractive about her.

She laughed as she switched positions on the bed, resting the selfie-stick on her knee. "Disappointed?"

He shook his head. "Not in the least."

Micah's Ember

She smiled as she took another sip of wine. "You don't have to lie, I don't mind. Things start to, um, *head south* as we age."

"Why do you do that?"

"Do what?"

"Act like you are past your prime or something. You're not old," he said.

She laughed. "Oh sweetie, trust me, thirty-nine is getting pretty old."

He made a clicking sound with his tongue as if he were waving off her comment. "Nonsense. If I didn't know how old you actually were, I would swear I was talking to someone my own age. You're beautiful, confident, and you have the same wacky sense of humor I do."

She blushed. "Well, thank you, but that doesn't change the fact I've packed on a few extra pounds over the years. Damn metabolism isn't what it used to be," she added with a laugh.

"Naw, you're soft and round, like a woman is supposed to be."

She raised an eyebrow. "I'm round? I'm not sure if that was meant as an insult or compliment."

He laughed nervously. "No, it was a compliment. I mean you're not a skinny little scarecrow who spends half her day in the gym building up muscle and the other half obsessing over what she's eating. There is no bigger turn-off for me than hugging a female that feels hard and stringy, especially if I take her out for a steak dinner and all she orders is lettuce with the dressing on the side."

She busted out laughing. "So you don't like fitness buffs or models then."

He grinned at her. "Hell no, I want a woman with a bit of meat on her bones so I don't feel like

Micah's Ember

I'm going to break her if I get a little rough in the bedroom."

Ember arched an eyebrow at his statement, her body instantly on fire as his words conjured up all kinds of erotic scenes inside her head. "So you like it rough, do you?"

A slow, playful smile slid across his face. "I believe that's my line."

"Mmm, yes, but I like to be the one giving the orders."

He squirmed around on the bed, his mouth slightly open. She could hear his breathing, labored, his eyes wide. "Really? Like, you're a top?"

She kept her bright blue eyes trained on his as she slowly nodded her head. "Yes," she said, her voice barely above a whisper. "Is that weird?"

"No," he said hoarsely, his hand moving off-screen.

Her eyes darted downward, her own breathing becoming labored. "Show me what you are doing, Micah," she said in a quiet, yet stern voice.

He gulped. "Yes ma'am," he whispered softly, the sound of his voice sending shivers down her spine.

He adjusted the angle of his phone, his hand soon coming into view where it rested over a raging hard-on which was trying desperately to escape the loose shorts he was wearing.

"Show me," she said, her voice once again raw with desire.

He pulled the waistband of his shorts down, slowly teasing her.

Her own eyes grew wide as she felt the now-familiar heat scorch its way down to settle in her center, her arousal so sudden and strong it was nearly painful. She fought the urge to groan as he slowly slid the shorts down, inch by delicious inch.

Micah's Ember

A loud pounding suddenly came through over the speakers of her tablet, and she heard Micah curse before the entire screen suddenly spun out of control before settling to show her a view of a white ceiling.

She heard muffled voices followed by the sound of a door closing close by. Suddenly, she saw Micah's face again, his cheeks flushed.

"Um, Spence just showed up. Apparently he's been trying to call for the last half-hour but I can't get incoming calls when I'm using Skipper."

"Everything okay?" she asked, silently wishing Spencer would take a long walk off a short pier, at least for tonight.

"Yeah, he just wants everyone in the studio for a quick practice session. We're so new, we've got to make sure this first big tour goes off without a hitch, you know? Sorry," he said, his aquamarine eyes still bright in his face.

"No problem. Go, have some fun for me too."

He grinned at her. "Call you tomorrow?"

She smiled back at him. "You better," she said before adding, "oh, and wear something sexy."

That beautifully seductive smile spread across his face again. "You too," he said softly before he hit the disconnect button, ending their strange conversation.

Ember rolled over on her bed, shoving her face into her pillow as she squealed in both happiness and frustration.

"*Fuck me!*" she screamed as she rolled onto her back, staring up at her ceiling with a lop-sided grin on her face. "What the fuck just happened?"

Micah's Ember

Chapter 4

Ember groaned as she tried to get her puffy eyes to focus on the alarm clock next to her bed. She had spent half the night pacing back and forth between her office and her bedroom, spending equal amounts of time prowling the internet for anything and everything dealing with both Micah and his band, *Tempered Souls*, and digging through her pathetically dated wardrobe and underwear drawer.

During that time she had discovered two things – the first being she didn't have a clue when Micah's birthday was and only had his word as to his true age, and second, she didn't have a damn thing in her closet she deemed even remotely "sexy". The closest thing she had which was the least bit "seductive" was a red, ill-fitting corset she had purchased off of a bidding site as part of a Halloween costume from five years ago. Even the few bra and panty sets still hiding out in her drawer had long since seen better days.

Deciding she was going to have to go to the store to restock her "sex-kitten" wardrobe, or at least something similar to it, she had finally settled into bed, determined to get an early start on shopping the next day. Unfortunately, sleep seemed elusive, and after tossing about in bed for more than two hours, she had given up and

Micah's Ember

opened her third bottle of wine, drinking herself into a stupor before practically passing out sometime around four in the morning.

Now, as the late morning sun tried to pry its way into her bedroom, she forced herself to roll out of bed and into the shower, standing under the hot water a bit longer than usual. Her dreams had been filled with images of Micah and all the wondrously naughty things she wanted to do to him. She was so damn horny, but she had refrained from gratifying herself, thus sending her overly aroused mind and body into a frenzy of lust-filled dreams.

She wasn't sure if Micah would even be up yet, but she didn't want to chance missing his call. She quickly sent him an instant message via Skipper, simply stating *gone shopping*. She quickly applied a smidge of eyeliner and mascara, brushing out her short, pixie-inspired hair and donning a wrap-dress before calling herself presentable enough to be seen in public.

She left the house in a hurry, slamming back a couple of aspirin to dull the insistent pounding in the back of her skull. One day she was going to realize she was getting way too old to keep knocking back the red wine like she had a habit of doing.

***

Ember eyed herself critically in the mirror. She had tried on no less than a dozen different combinations of bras, panties, corsets, and any number of assorted teddies and other lingerie. She had tried them with and without support garments, whole pieces, two pieces, some with garter belts, some without, and yet no matter what she stuffed her ass into, she couldn't help but feel

Micah's Ember

her thighs were too big, her stomach too flabby, and her ass too saggy to catch the eye of anyone, much less the drummer of an up-and-coming rock band who was nearly half her age.

"What the actual fuck am I doing?" she asked herself softly. Did she really think Micah even remotely liked her? He had probably told his bandmates what had transpired between them, all of them having a good laugh at her expense. The mere thought of what all could have been said about her made her sick to her stomach. She had to be insane to think anything more would happen outside of what had transpired between them last night.

It also begged the question of how many other women he had struck up this same conversation with since joining *Tempered Souls*. How many "fans" was he conversing with on a regular basis who thought they were the only ones chatting with him? Did he make a habit of doing this? Did he find some sort of perverse pleasure in making women fall all over themselves thinking they were special because he was talking to them? How many more on-cam conversations had he had after hanging up with her?

And so what if nothing else happened? What if she was only one in a whole line of women he chatted with? It was all in good fun, right? So long as she didn't let herself get involved, it was just something fun and interesting. No harm, no foul.

Sighing, she debated on actually purchasing any of the lingerie. She could pay her bills but it left very little for splurging, which was the main reason why she stayed at home all the time.

Deciding it wouldn't hurt to get a few new things for some of her burlesque-inspired selfies, she finally decided on a new red corset which actually fit along with a form-fitting black one piece

Micah's Ember

teddy designed to wear under tight dresses sans underwear. Four hours later, after treating herself to a new pair of fuck-me heels as well as a deliciously sinful iced coffee, she stumbled through her front door. She was exhausted but oddly happy. She knew even if she never heard another word out of Micah, she would never forget his infectious smile or continue to be quite so hard on herself if she slipped up and had an extra roll with dinner.

Chapter 5

Ember yawned, standing up to stretch after spending the last three hours binge watching one of her favorite series. She still had two complete seasons to go, but it would be worth it once she finally got caught up to the current season. It would be nice to carry on an actual conversation with Nicci without having to cover her ears periodically while she screamed, "I haven't watched that episode yet!"

It was getting late, and as she had suspected, she had not heard a single word out of Micah. He hadn't replied to her instant message inside of Skipper, he had not messaged her on Snapagram, nor had he sent her anything through Instachat. Trying not to feel too bad about it, she decided to take a hot bath and try on some of her new outfits. If nothing else, she could at least get a few new selfies posted on her Snapagram account.

Two glasses of wine and an hour later, she finished lacing herself up into her new red corset and black lace miniskirt, finishing the outfit off with her new fuck-me stilettos. Feeling better about her body than she had in a really long time, she arranged herself on the bed and began to take a few snapshots, adding them to her Snapagram feed. Within a few minutes the posts had a few

Micah's Ember

dozen hearts each, as her porn-inspired photos generally did.

Just as she posed herself to take her final selfie of the night, her Skipper app suddenly opened up, announcing she had an incoming call from Micah.

Smiling, she hit the accept button, the phone still hovering a few feet above her, giving a nice view of her body sprawled out on her bed.

"Holy fuck!" he exclaimed as she came into view on his phone.

"What?" she asked sweetly.

He blinked a few times, his mouth slightly agape as his eyes roamed over her body. "Damn, woman, warn me next time. I wasn't expecting a show first thing."

She laughed. "Well, you sort of interrupted me."

His happy smile slowly disappeared from his face. "Ohhh, so you have company?"

She began laughing in earnest then. The look on his face was just so damn precious, she wanted to squeeze him. "No, I'm alone. I was taking some photos for my Snapagram feed."

Just as soon as his smile had disappeared, it suddenly returned as his entire face lit up at her words. "New photos? When are you posting them?"

She grinned. "I've already uploaded most of them. But," she said as she paused long enough to flip through some of the photos and send them to his Skipper account via instant message, "there are a few that are a bit too revealing for my account."

She watched as Micah scrolled through his messages, his aquamarine eyes growing wide as the edges of those luscious lips slowly turned up into a seductive smile. "Damn," was all he said as his eyes drank in the candid photos she had just sent him.

Micah's Ember

"I take it you like them then?" she asked, a half-smile still on her face.

He nodded as his eyes darted back and forth between the photos in his messenger and her live feed still streaming through his phone.

She laughed. "So, what are you up to tonight?"

"Been practicing."

"Again?" she asked before she rolled her eyes. "That was stupid, forget I said it. I keep forgetting you guys are going on the road, so of course you are practicing." She paused as she laughed. "Anything else going on?"

The screen moved as he shifted positions, sitting back on his bed. "Naw, Spence is an absolute *monster* when it comes to practice sessions. We've been in his basement since early this morning."

Her eyes widened. "*Damn*, that long?" She shook her head. "I bet you are wiped out."

He shrugged, his eyes looking sleepy as he gazed at her. "It's tiring, but I'm good. I was afraid you had went to sleep already. I actually bailed on the rest of the guys so I could come home to chat with you."

She arched one perfectly plucked eyebrow. "Oh?"

He nodded his head slowly. "Yeah," he said, his voice low.

"Did you do what I asked you to?" she asked, her voice equally low.

He looked confused for a moment. "Sorry, I don't know?"

She chuckled low in her throat. "Did you wear something sexy for me?"

He blinked at her before giving her a sheepish grin. "Um, not really. I hopped in the shower as soon as I walked in the door."

Micah's Ember

Her smile widened. "Hmm, so here I am all dolled up and you're sitting around in your bath robe." She clucked her tongue. "Someone is already being a naughty boy."

He stuck her tongue out at her, an act which only made her want to shove her tongue down his throat. "Now what have I told you about doing that?" she asked.

"That some cougar is going to shove her tongue down my throat if I keep sticking my tongue out."

She nodded her head slowly. "Mmm, hmm."

He looked at her wide-eyed. "Is that a promise?"

"Oh, yes, darlin', and I always keep my promises."

He smiled again, his eyes practically twinkling in his face, but he remained silent.

"So, what are you wearing then?" she asked again.

"You wanna see?"

She nodded slowly, her lashes lowered as he moved his phone slowly down the length of his body. His grey t-shirt stretched across broad shoulders, the camera moving agonizingly slow as he moved it further down until finally she caught sight of the tight red boxer-briefs he was currently wearing.

Ember nearly groaned aloud as she saw the bulge nestled there. She was already on a slow burn, but seeing his young body sprawled out on his bed and the tantalizing outline of his cock caused the searing heat to ignite into a raging inferno, the warmth immediately spreading down her own body, a sensation which was both painful and pleasurable at the same time.

Micah moved his phone back so he could see Ember, the lustful look on her face making him

Micah's Ember

oddly euphoric. He was a bit self-conscious about his body. He spent long hours either in the studio practicing, writing music, or recording, topped off by months on the road. After a few years of fast food takeout and not nearly enough exercise, he thought his body wasn't in nearly the shape it should have been. It wasn't even in as good of shape as it had been just a year ago, back when he was regularly going to the gym. Seeing the lust on Ember's face, however, gave him one hell of a rush. It was nice to know someone found him attractive.

"Like what you see?"

"Fuck yeah," she whispered as she trailed her fingertips down the small swell of her breasts, her hand disappearing out of the camera frame.

"What are you doing?" he asked teasingly, his own hand moving down to his crotch. She still had her phone in the selfie-stick, giving him a view of the majority of her body, a sight which he found extremely arousing. Her small breasts were prominently on display in her tight-fitting corset, her shapely legs looking especially sexy in her black stilettos. She looked so delicate and feminine, he kept imaging what it would be like to feel her milky-white flesh beneath his fingertips.

She smiled. "Wishing you didn't live half-way across the damn country, to be honest," she said with a light laugh.

"Really? Rather be here with me?" he asked as he held his phone further away, allowing her to watch as he slowly ran his hand over the growing bulge in his shorts.

She nodded again, her breathing slightly labored as she eyed him hungrily.

"What would you do if you were here right now?" he asked.

"Screw you six ways from Sunday," she said hoarsely, her eyes watching his hand intently.

Micah's Ember

"Mmm, is that another promise?"

"Oh hell yeah," she said as she ripped her eyes away from his crotch.

She rolled over suddenly, the image on his screen bouncing around until it settled a few seconds later, her body now sitting in the center of her bed. "Take off your shirt," she said as she poked one finger in her mouth, her teeth nibbling lightly on the end of the nail.

He did as he was told, his face and chest coming back into view a few seconds later as he settled back on his bed.

"Your turn," he said teasingly as he propped his head up on his arm.

She raised an eyebrow. "Are you sure you want to see?" she asked.

He laughed. "Hell yeah I want to see, why would you ask?"

"Okay, but if you have nightmares you can't say I didn't warn you," she said with a chuckle. It wasn't that she minded showing him, but she seriously feared he would be permanently scarred for life if she did.

"Nonsense. You show me yours and I'll show you mine."

She gave him a lop-sided grin. "That's not how this works," she said.

"Mmm, then how does it work?"

She moved her hands to slowly cup her breasts, her fingers moving lightly across the tops. "You show me yours first."

"That hardly seems fair," he said, his eyes watching as her hands massaged the soft mounds of flesh, squeezing them together before releasing them. He watched in fascination as the small orbs bounced inside the tight corset. He could see the outline of her taunt nipples through the thin cloth,

Micah's Ember

a sight which caused his breath to catch in his throat.

She reached behind her back and unclasped the hooks holding the garment together, one hand holding the fabric in place. She let it fall from her body, her hands cupping her breasts and keeping them hidden from view at the same time.

"No fair," he whispered, not sure if he were more jealous of her hands cupping those firm orbs or the bed she was slowly grinding herself against.

"Touch yourself, Micah," she said softly, her hands still massaging the tender mounds of her breasts. "Pretend it's me."

His eyes watched her hands as they cupped her flesh, her taunt nipples coming into view for an all-too brief moment. "What would you do to me if you were here?" he asked, his dick so hard he thought for sure he'd end up at the hospital before the night was over with.

"I'd start at the top, slowly kissing my way down, nibbling at your skin, until my hands reached your hard cock," she said breathlessly as she ran her own hands down the sides of her body, her arms pushing her breasts together as her right hand shoved her ruffled skirt further up her thighs, her hand disappearing inside the flimsy lace G-string she wore underneath.

His breath caught in his throat, his dick twitching in his shorts at the sight of her body, her tits small but still perfectly round and firm. The sound of her sultry voice was enough to drive him insane as she continued to describe in tantalizing detail what she wanted to do to him.

"Then what?" he asked eagerly, his voice breathless.

"I'd wrap my hand around you, pop the head of your cock into my mouth, swirl my tongue around your cockhead slowly before allowing my

Micah's Ember

lips to slide down the length of you, inch by delicious inch, until I had all of you shoved down my throat. And then I'd allow you to slide back out, and then back in, over and over again, faster and faster until you begged me to stop."

His hand mimicked what she was describing, his fist squeezing his dick, her vivid details only making him hornier.

"What if you couldn't get all of me into your mouth?" he asked.

She smiled, groaning slightly as she squeezed one of her breasts with her hand while the other moved around inside her panties. He watched her eagerly, wishing she was there so he could rip the offending fabric away from her body.

"What makes you think I couldn't swallow all of your cock?" she asked.

"I'm a pretty big guy," he said with a smirk.

She tilted her head to the side, her half-closed lids suddenly flying open. She grinned at him. "Really? Show me."

"Mmm, I'm not sure you could handle it," he said teasingly.

"Show me, Micah," she said, her voice low and demanding.

"Yes ma'am," he said, loving the thrill of excitement which shivered down his spine as he said the words.

He moved his phone down, the sight of his hard cock jutting out from the band of his boxers making the burning heat inside of her rage out of control. She gasped, her eyes wide as she stared at him.

"Holy fuck me running, you weren't kidding," she said huskily, unable to stop herself from running her tongue along her lips.

He chuckled at the look on her face, loving how she stared at him like a woman starved. "You

Micah's Ember

think you could get all of this down that slender throat of yours?" he asked as he grasped the base of his cock.

She nodded, her eyes still glued to his engorged member. "Hell yeah, or I'd choke myself trying."

He laughed again, his sleepy aquamarine eyes shining brightly in the dull light.

"I'd love to see your lips wrapped around my dick right now," he whispered as his hand began slowly caressing the length of his cock.

She groaned lightly as she watched. "Mmm, I'd love to suck your dick. I want to feel it in the back of my throat as it slides in and out, slowly at first, then faster and faster-"

A sudden pounding on Micah's door caused both of them to stop as Micah turned toward the noise.

"Were you expecting company?" she asked, her hands moving to cover her breasts.

"No," he said, his head still turned, his brow furrowed as he secretly willed whoever the fuck was at his front door to go away.

"Are you going to answer it?" she asked.

He stayed still, one hand still wrapped around his cock. "Not if I can keep from it," he said.

They both waited for what felt like forever, but less than a minute later the pounding came again, more insistent this time.

"Dammit!" they both said at the same time.

Micah turned back to his phone, grinning at her. "Fuck, I guess I better get that before they wake up the whole damn neighborhood."

"Okay," she said.

"Mind hanging on for a sec until I find out what's going on?"

She nodded. "Sure, just don't leave me hanging," she said with a grin.

Micah's Ember

He returned her smile. "Never," he said as he placed his phone face-down on his bed. She could hear him jerking on his pants, grunting as he shoved himself into the confining fabric. A few seconds later she heard the door to his bedroom open and close quietly, followed by the sounds of muffled voices.

Finally, after several minutes had passed, he picked up his phone again, his face looking unhappy. "It's Spence again. Everyone is headed over to Nik's for a few drinks. They insist I come with."

She sighed before nodding, trying not to look like a love-struck cougar who was losing her favorite toy. "Sounds like fun. You should go, have a few drinks for me."

"You sure?" he asked, the expression on his face so adorable she wished like hell she could kiss him.

"Yes, I'm sure," she said with a laugh. "I don't expect you to sit around your house keeping me company. We can chat later. Besides," she added as she hugged her pillow tighter, "I get the feeling Spence isn't one to take 'no' for an answer."

He grinned at her, both grateful she wasn't acting like a jealous bitch but also disappointed their little 'chat' was ending on unfinished business. "You are definitely right about that," he said, pulling his phone to his chest as Spence came into his bedroom.

"For fuck's sake, Micah, what the hell is taking so long? The guys are waiting. Who are you talking to in here?"

"None of your business," he said as he motioned for Spence to leave the room. "I'll be out in a minute, just hold on a sec, okay?"

"Okay, man, but hurry up will ya?"

Micah's Ember

Micah waited until his friend was out of the room before he pulled his phone back out. "Damn, I gotta go. Are you going to be up later?"

She glanced at the time on her phone. It was already damn near three in the morning. "Can't say for sure, but you can call me whenever you want, 'kay?"

He nodded. "Okay, fair enough. Chat you soon?"

She smiled at him. "You better," she said as she suddenly tossed the pillow aside, the camera on her phone showing her sitting completely naked on her bed.

"Goodnight, Micah," she said softly before she clicked *disconnect* on her Skipper app, her image disappearing from his phone.

"Holy fuck me," he whispered.

Micah's Ember

Chapter 6

Ember tossed around in her bed for the next two hours, unable to sleep. She was so tempted to pull out her favorite dildo and end the burning desire surging through her body. She needed the release, but no matter how much she teased herself, she just couldn't let herself go. All she could think about was Micah and that huge cock of his, the images of him shoved deep inside of her making her ache with lust. She wished like hell they lived closer, that their tour would bring them within a few hundred miles of her. She had never wanted anyone this badly before, and she wasn't quite sure she liked the sensation. What the fuck was wrong with her?

Finally giving up on trying to get any sleep, she tossed off the covers and went to brush her teeth, shedding her tight corset and G-string in favor of a custom ripped *Tempered Souls* shirt and a pair of bikini panties. She poured herself a cup of coffee and settled down at her computer, intent upon catching up with her photography editing.

Nearly an hour later, her *Skipper* app went off, indicating she had an inbound call from Micah. She clicked on the *accept* button, Micah's sleepy face popping up on her twenty-two inch monitor.

"You're up?" he asked, sounding surprised.

Micah's Ember

She smiled. "Well, technically I've never been to sleep so yeah, I'm up."

He laughed. "Maybe I should have phrased that differently. Maybe I should have asked if you are *still* up."

A slow, naughty smile slid across her face. "Yes, but a better question is, are *you* still up?"

He stared at her for a second before he realized what she was implying. He chuckled. "As a matter of fact, I am. Couldn't really sleep. I kept having visions of red corsets and firm tits dancing in my head."

"Is that so?" she asked.

"Yes," he said.

"Yes *ma'am*," she corrected, her voice a bit low as she continued to smile at him.

"So that's the way it's going to be?" he asked, one eyebrow arched.

She slowly nodded her head. "Mmm, hmm. It's yes ma'am or no ma'am. And you don't get to touch yourself unless you ask for permission first. That is, if you are into that kind of kink." She paused for a second before she asked, "So tell me, are you into that kind of thing?"

He slowly nodded. "Yes ma'am," he said quietly, his voice low and eager.

She smiled, wondering how far he was willing to take this relationship. "Now, where were we?" She asked as she sat back in her chair, giving him a better view of her braless torso in the shredded band tee-shirt which barely covered her tits. She reached up, one hand softly teasing her nipple.

His eyes grew round, locking on to her bouncing breasts as she lounged in her chair. "Umm...," his voice trailed off, his brain unable to concentrate on much of anything with her hand playing with the soft, rounded mounds of flesh.

Micah's Ember

"Ah, yes, I remember now. I believe I was telling you what I wanted to do to you if I were there."

He nodded his head again, his eyes still watching her hand. "Yes ma'am, I believe you said something about sucking my cock until I begged you to stop," he said, his words causing such lustful visions to dance through his head that he shuddered.

"Mmm, hmm," she purred, one hand still pinching her nipple as her other moved off camera to trace slow, lazy circles around her clit. "I want to feel your cock in my throat as I run my tongue along the top, feel you slip further and further inside until you can't take it anymore."

His breath was slightly labored as he watched her, his own hand once again mimicking her words.

"What did I say?" she asked, her voice low but stern as she watched his hand move toward his crotch.

He immediately stopped. "May I?" he asked timidly, feeling unsure of what he should do.

"Show me, Micah," she said, her voice low and husky.

"Yes ma'am," he said as he shoved his boxers down so she could watch him as he stroked his cock.

"Fuck, I wish I was there," she whispered, her hips undulating slightly as her arousal increased. She had already soaked through her thin cotton panties, and she was just getting started.

"I wish you were, too," he replied, his hands still slowly stroking his cock as he watched her.

"I want to see," he said hoarsely, the sight of her hand moving around inside her undies just off camera was driving him insane.

Micah's Ember

She shook her head slowly. "Not yet, not until you come for me."

His hand slowed down as his eyes grew a bit wider in his face. "You want me to come? But then the fun would be over."

She smiled at him. "Oh no, sweetie, the fun would just be getting started."

He blinked a few times. "Umm, so are you saying you *like it* to last a long time? Please tell me you like multiple orgasms."

She slowly nodded. "Yes. One or two is just going to piss me off. Are you up for multiples, or would you rather just stick to one?"

"Oh fuck yes, please, multiple times, please?"

She chuckled. "Multiple times for you or me?"

"Um, both, please?"

Her smile broadened. "Strip, Micah. I want to see all of you," she said.

"Yes, ma'am," he answered eagerly, setting his phone down for the thirty seconds it took him to shrug out of his tee shirt and boxers. He rummaged around in his nightstand for his tube of lube while he was at it, rubbing a generous amount in his palm. He settled back on the bed, dick in one hand and his phone in the other, ready to pick things back up where they left off.

He stopped, his aquamarine eyes round in his face as he saw Ember sitting at her desk, her top gone, one leg slung over the arm of her chair as she continued to massage one perfectly round tit while her other hand teased her soaked inner folds.

"Keep going, Micah," she demanded. "Pretend it's me touching you. Imagine it's me stroking that delicious cock, slowly, squeezing just the tiniest bit as my hand moves down."

He groaned, his eyes half-closed as his hand moved along his length, the slow, steady strokes

Micah's Ember

increasing every few seconds. "Fuck, I wish you were really here, I'd love to lick your pussy while you suck my cock."

"Mmm," she moaned, her tongue licking her lips. "My naughty boy likes sixty-nine?"

"Yes. I bet you taste like honey."

"Not really. I'm tangy, like lemons."

He groaned again. "How the fuck do you know what you taste like?"

She giggled. "You think I've never sucked a dick after it's fucked me?"

His hand slowed. "You actually do that?"

She nodded. "Oh, sweetie, I've done some things that would probably make your hair curl up. Great thing about an older woman. We're not nearly as hung up on trying out new things."

"Damn, woman, you keep this up and I'm going to have to fly to Louisiana just so I can taste you for myself."

"No fair tasting unless you plan to fuck me good and proper afterwards."

His hand was working faster, his eyes watching as she inched her panties down just a tad. "Come for me, Micah. I want to see you come, then I'm going to come for you."

"*Fuck*," he hissed, his eyes watching her hands working inside her panties as he jerked his dick faster and faster, the tingling inside his balls mounting so quickly he barely had time to do much more than gasp before he blew his load.

"Mmm, *fuck me*, Micah. No fair, I wish I was there to taste it."

He groaned, his closed eyes opening just in time to see her sitting naked in her chair, one leg still draped over the side. He watched as her finger rubbed circles around her clit, her hips moving in time with her hand as her other pinched her pink nipple.

Micah's Ember

"Holy, fuck, Ember, you are gorgeous. I want to taste that sweet pussy of yours, lick your clit while I finger you until you come in my mouth."

"Yes!" she purred, her eyes watching as he began to stroke his still hard cock once again. "Then I want you to fuck me, Micah, hard and fast."

"Oh fuck yes," he hissed, the tingling inside of him building quicker than before.

"Fuck, I'm going to come," she moaned, feeling the beginnings of her release shoot up the inside of her thighs before the orgasm ripped through her body, her head tossed back as she groaned his name.

She rode out her release, her fingers working her clit as her back arched, his name on her lips as the pleasure rippled through her entire core like multi-colored waves. She watched him through her lashes as he came again, his hips thrust forward as he did.

A good minute-and-a-half later, she slowly came down from her orgasm-induced haze, his eyes locked on her, his mouth slightly agape.

"Holy. *Fuck.*"

She blinked, not really sure how to take his wide-eyed stare. She glanced down, realizing she had completely soaked her desk chair. She would have blushed, but she was so used to it all she could do was smile. "Sorry, guess I probably should have warned you about that beforehand."

He slowly shook his head. "Oh no, that was legit one of the best damn kept secrets you could have."

"So you're not completely disgusted?"

He shook his head. "Fuck no. It just makes me want to make you come in person so I can see it firsthand."

Micah's Ember

She giggled. "I'm surprised you even know what a squirter is, much less find it attractive."

"Who the hell you been screwing all these years? What man doesn't think that's sexy as fuck?"

She shrugged. "A lot, apparently. Still single, remember?"

He reached over to grab his shirt, using it to clean the pearly droplets of cum from his hand and dick. "Then you have been dating some serious assholes, babe. I'd fuck you all night long just to see how many towels we'd go through."

She laughed. "You are something else, darlin'."

He grinned. "You are too, my sweet Ember."

He groaned as he caught sight of the time. "Damn, it's nearly nine and we've got rehearsal in a few hours."

"Need to go?" she asked, trying not to pout.

"Ugh, *yes*, unfortunately," he replied.

"'Kay, call me when you get a chance?"

"You know it. You going to be up later?"

"I'll probably take a nap, but I've got work tomorrow so I'll probably go to bed around ten."

He nodded. "Okay, I'll try to hit you up before then. Give you a little something to help you sleep better."

She groaned, his words causing her already aching pussy to throb with unbridled lust. "I'm holding you to that," she said with a laugh.

"Then it's a date," he said, his plump lips turned up in a lop-sided grin. "See you later."

"Goodnight, Micah," she said.

"Goodnight, Ember."

Micah's Ember

Chapter 7

She had planned to take a nap, but her brain wouldn't quiet down long enough for her to finally slip over the edge into oblivion. Giving up on getting any rest, she dragged herself out of bed and got dressed, deciding to drive the nearly fifty miles to one of her favorite fetish stores to stock up on some new toys. On the off chance whatever-the-hell had just happened between her and Micah continued, she wanted to buy something really sexy to wear for him tonight.

Ember arrived at her destination in less than an hour, taking her time as she browsed through the racks of fetish wear, heels, corsets, whips, adult toys, bondage gear, and jewelry.

She wasn't quite sure how far into any of this Micah would be willing to go, if he even called her again that was, but she couldn't help but secretly hope he was *really* into this kinky-ass shit as much as she was. Two hours later, she walked back to her car loaded down with boxes and bags filled with new outfits and a few cute items she planned to mail to Micah – *if* he ever called her again, of course.

She tried not to think about the money she had just spent, reminding herself she still had an entertainment budget even if she had been saving it for the better part of a year. There was no harm

Micah's Ember

in treating herself every once in a while. Honestly, it felt good to get out of the house and buy something for herself for once. She was so focused on her career she had put all her own needs and wants on hold indefinitely.

Ember stopped off at a local restaurant to grab a bite to eat, opting for a tasty salad which probably had as many calories in it as a hamburger and fries. Even if it did, at least she didn't feel guilty about eating it.

She guessed she might also want to invest in a new treadmill and see if she could at least try to put her sagging ass back where it once was, especially if *Tempered Souls* ever played a show close enough so she could actually meet Micah. Seeing her on camera where she controlled the lighting and camera angel was one thing, but being sprawled out on a bed in the flesh with all her jelly rolls front-and-center may not be nearly as attractive to him as her on-screen persona.

The thought of seeing the broad-shouldered, incredibly sexy drummer whose dick just begged to be sucked sent a shiver of desire down her spine and a searing heat spreading between her legs. She had never wanted to fuck someone so badly in her life. Watching him stroking that absolutely amazing cock of his made her squirm around in her car seat as she raced to get home.

***

Just before eight-thirty her Skipper app announced an incoming call from Micah. She tried to control the fluttering of her heart as her most intimate areas immediately began to ache at the thought of him. She quickly hit the *accept* button

Micah's Ember

on the app, unable to wipe the huge smile off her lips as his gorgeous face suddenly filled the screen.

"Hey there cutie," she said as she settled back in her bed.

"Hey yourself," he replied, those luscious lips of his curled up into a lop-sided grin. His eyes narrowed a bit as his smile increased. "What are you wearing?" he asked as he moved his phone closer to his face.

She giggled. "Um, well, I kinda might have went shopping at one of my favorite fetish stores," she said as she ran her hands over her breasts and down a body squeezed into a latex corset-type body suit.

"Oh you did, did you?" he asked with a chuckle. "Sounds like fun, and I'm a wee bit jealous. So what all did you buy? Do I get to see?"

"All kinds of neat and fun things," she replied, feeling herself flush. It was time to see just how kinky this kid *really* was.

She moved her phone further away, letting him see the bodysuit she was wearing. It was black and fit like a second skin. It was strapless and pushed her tits up and together to create the illusion of a larger bust. Cut high around the legs, it looked a lot like a latex one-piece bathing suit, except there was a zipper running through the crotch from right above her pubic bone all the way to the back, stopping right above the swell of her ass cheeks. It was what was called an "easy-access" panel opening, and was designed to allow the wearer to be fucked in whichever hole they preferred, all without having to take the bodysuit off.

He whistled as he saw her outfit, leaning back as his eyes soaked in the sight of her. "Hot damn, woman, that outfit is sexy as fuck."

"You like it?" she asked, smiling in relief.

Micah's Ember

"Hell yeah, what man in his right mind wouldn't like it?"

She shrugged. "I guess I'm just not used to anyone your age being into any of this kinky shit. Hell, most men *my age* aren't into any of this kinky shit. You, sir, are quite the rare find."

He grinned. "You have no idea how kinky I can be."

"Hmmm, now you have me completely captivated. I'd love to find out just how kinky your mind really is."

He just smiled at her as he asked, "So what else did you buy? Got a few whips and chains in one of those bags?"

She giggled. "I may have bought a flogger or two," she said, reaching out of frame and grabbing a shopping bag. She rummaged inside of it, drawing out a small flogger. She drew it across her hand before smacking it into her palm, gazing at him through her lashes as she did.

He squirmed a bit as he watched her, making her entire body tingle with excitement. She wasn't sure which turned her on more, the thought of dominating someone so young, or the thought of someone his age being her own personal Dom.

Shuddering with excitement, she pulled out a small butt plug which had a plume of multi-colored feathers on one end. She held it up, a smirk on her face. She couldn't wait to find out if he knew what it was, and if not, oh what fun she was going to have teaching him.

"What the hell is that thing?" he asked.

She grinned. Oh yeah, so much fun. "It's a butt plug, sweetie. When inserted, it makes the wearer look like they have a lovely feathered plume, like a tail. They come in all kinds of different looks, everything from a horse tail to a tiger tail. I personally like the feathers the best

Micah's Ember

because they are not heavy so they don't pull down on the plug when wearing it. Plus the tickling of the feathers against your naked ass is really quit exhilarating."

She watched him closely as she explained all this to him, waiting to see if he would suddenly make some excuse to jump off the call. In her experience, when it came to anal play, men fell into two categories – they were either all for it or all against it. She had yet to find anyone who was on the fence about it. They either fantasized about it, wanted to do it, or the thought of it stopped them dead in their tracks.

She really hoped Micah fell into the former category, and in all honesty she was a bit worried he would think she was thoroughly disgusting for being into it. But as his eyes grew wider and his breathing quickened with excitement, she was beginning to wonder if there was anything she could do which would be an actual turn-off for him.

She paused as she looked him straight in the eye. "Are you scared yet?"

He slowly shook his head. "Hell no. Horny as fuck, but not scared. I don't supposed you have some anal beads in there as well?"

She grinned. "I already have a set of anal beads, including some that vibrate," she whispered, resisting the urge to ask him if he wanted them for her, or for himself.

"*Fuck*," he groaned, shifting positions in bed as all the naughty images danced inside his head. His hand moved down to rub at his crotch, Ember's eyes immediately moving to see what he was doing.

"What did I say about touching yourself?" she asked, her voice low but demanding.

Micah immediately stopped, moving his hand away from his aching cock. "Sorry," he mumbled.

Micah's Ember

She shook her head. "No, I asked you a question. What did I say about touching yourself?" she asked again, a bit more stern.

He swallowed, but his breathing was becoming even more erratic as he wiggled around on the bed again. "I'm not allowed without asking first," he answered, his eyes boring into hers.

She nodded her head slowly. "That's right. You're being naughty. And since I'm not there to properly punish my naughty boy, the only recourse I have is to withhold your release. Understand?"

He slowly nodded his head. "Yes, ma'am," he said hoarsely.

She smiled again. "Good boy. Now where were we?"

He squirmed around in the bed again, his nails digging into his hand to stop himself from reaching for his dick. "Umm, so what else you got hiding in that little bag of tricks of yours? May I see?"

A slow, evilly seductive smile spread across her face. If the butt plug didn't faze him, she couldn't wait to see what his reaction would be to this new toy.

"Oh, something I've been wanting to buy for a while now, just didn't see the point of getting it without someone around to use it," she said, reaching into the paper bag and pulling out another whip. This one had a twelve-inch rubberized handle that was nearly five-inches in diameter with slightly raised ribbing.

"That's a rather odd looking whip," he said as he watched her wrap her hand around it.

"It's not just a whip," she said softly as she began to move the handle of the whip slowly through her enclosed hand.

His sleepy eyes grew wide as he realized why the handle was so large and ribbed. "Ohhh," he

Micah's Ember

said hoarsely, his mind immediately conjuring up images of himself using the handle on her, wondering just how much of those twelve inches he could manage to work inside her tight body. He shivered, the thought of everything he wanted to do to her making him so horny he could barely stand it.

"I have a few more outfits, but I'll save those for another night. Oh," she added, digging around inside the bag again.

She pulled out a small square box, opening it to pull out what was inside. She held it up to the camera on her phone, showing the leather and silver bracelet to Micah.

"What is it?" he asked.

"It's a gift for you, in the event you ever decide you want it that is," she replied.

"What's that written on it?"

"It's a bracelet," she answered. "Specifically, it's a slave bracelet, and it's engraved with the words OWNED BY MISTRESS." She put the bracelet back in the box, nestling it inside the tiny cocoon of tissue paper. "As I said, I bought it as a gift for you. It's up to you whether or not you want it. I'll not speak of it again," she said as she set it back inside the box. "Just keep in mind it's there, and if you ever want it all you have to do is ask."

She set the bag to the side, once again smiling at him. "Now, you've seen what I'm wearing, and all of my new toys. It's your turn," she said softly as she leaned back against the pile of pillows on her bed, spreading her legs just a bit so he could see the easy-access zipper in the crotch of her outfit. "Show me what you're wearing."

He grinned, ducking his head as he blushed. "I'm afraid I'm not exactly dressed for the occasion," he said as he showed her the tee-shirt and loose fitting shorts he was wearing. "I've never

Micah's Ember

really had any need for wearing anything other than jeans and tee-shirts."

She smiled as she ran her fingertips lightly across the swell of her breasts. "No, you look very sexy," she whispered as she eyed the bulge inside his shorts. "But you should never wear a shirt around me," she continued, one hand moving to grasp the zipper in her bodysuit. "I love looking at you, love to see you grasping your cock." She inched the zipper down as she talked, her voice low and mesmerizing.

He discovered his own hand moving to his twitching dick, shoving the waistband of his shorts and underwear out of his way before he stopped, realizing what he was about to do. He looked up at her, watching as she unzipped the opening in the crotch of her suit inch by tantalizing inch until he was finally rewarded with a view of her already dripping pussy. He swallowed, loving that she looked like a living sex doll, his own little plaything which he ached to touch.

"Take your shirt off," she demanded in a soft whisper, the tips of her fingers running lazy circles around her opening.

He sat up long enough to take off his shirt, his hands pausing before he removed his shorts. "May I take off my shorts, too?" he asked, his voice husky.

"Yes," she whispered in answer, reaching under her pillow to pull out a small, silver bullet-shaped item.

"What's that?" he asked.

"This," she said as she flicked a switch on one end, "is what we women refer to as a 'Silver Bullet.' It's basically a woman's best friend, at least when it comes to the bedroom."

Micah's Ember

He watched as she placed the small vibrating thing against her clit, her body immediately jerking in response. "*Fuck*," she hissed as she groaned.

He moved to grasp his dick again, but stopped. "May I touch myself?" he asked, a bit unsure of what he should do.

He had read about the dom/sub lifestyle on many sites, had watched stories unfold on more than a few forums. But none of that could actually prepare someone who wanted to enter into this type of relationship in the real world, especially when that relationship was pretty much nothing but a virtual one.

"Yes, I want you to stroke your cock and watch me, pretend you are doing everything to my body, pretend it is your hands touching me, your cock fucking me."

"Yes, ma'am," he whispered as he settled back, eagerly teasing his own cock as he watched her.

She moved the little vibrating bullet in slow circles around her swollen clit, her breathing quickly becoming labored as the ache inside of her grew. "Talk to me, Micah, tell me what you want to see."

He licked his lips. Damn, she was sexy as hell and he could hardly believe she was sprawled out on her bed putting on a show just for him. "I want you to show me how your new whip works," he said, his voice low and husky.

She didn't answer, merely picked up the whip and ran the rounded tip of the handle around the outside of her slippery opening. "Tell me how you would fuck me, Micah. I want to hear you telling me what you would like to do to me."

He nearly groaned, the thought of being there with her and doing all of these things *to* her rather than just watching via webcam made his dick

Micah's Ember

twitch and ache with desire. "Slip it inside, Ember, slowly. I want to see how deep you can get it."

She moaned as she teased the outside of her slit before sliding the tip of the handle into her soft, pink folds, working it in and out slowly, moving it deeper and deeper inside of her tight confines until finally her body could not take another inch of it.

"Keep going, please. I want to watch you fuck yourself with it."

She slid the dildo handle in and out of her wet cavern, the combination of the ribbed texture and the vibrating bullet on her clit driving her mad with desire. Within just a few seconds she had worked up a quick pace, managing to move the handle deeper and deeper each time she thrust it within her tight, wet opening.

Micah watched enthralled, his own hand squeezing his dick as he worked it faster and faster, feeling the tingling inside his balls building up at an alarming rate.

"Ember, I'm going to come."

"*No*," she commanded. "Not until I tell you to, understand?"

He moaned, but immediately replied, "Yes, ma'am."

She continued to fuck herself with the handle of the whip, her hips moving in time with each thrust. "I'm going to come, Micah, and when I do I want you to come, too."

"Yes, ma'am," he replied again. His voice was low and hoarse as he watched her in eager anticipation as she bucked her hips upward, moaning his name as she suddenly came, her sweet juices soaking the spread beneath her.

"*Fuck*," he hissed, the tingling inside his balls building up before he spilt over the edge, imagining himself buried balls-deep inside of her sweet pussy as it pulsed around him.

Micah's Ember

The two of them lay still for a few seconds, their breathing erratic as they tried to regain control of their bodies. He watched her through half-closed lids, finding the image of her with the handle still shoved deep inside her dripping center one of the sexiest damn things he had ever seen. It made him wonder what she would look like bent over with the cute feathers displayed on her upturned ass.

"Next time, can you wear the feather tail?" he asked, his voice breathless.

She smiled. "Absolutely. Maybe I'll buy you one too and mail it to you," she said, her blue eyes twinkling.

His lips turned up at the corners as he stared at her still sprawled out on the bed. "I'll message you my address."

Micah's Ember

Chapter 8

Monday morning came all too soon, as it always did. Ember slowly dragged herself out of bed nearly an hour late, rushing through her morning routine quicker than she would have liked. She had sat up chatting with Micah until nearly midnight, making her normal five A.M. wakeup call practically impossible to adhere to.

She and Micah had discussed their lives in great detail, and she was oddly pleased they had a lot more in common than she had originally thought. They liked a lot of the same bands, they liked the same types of movies, and they both had considered journalism as a profession. Music was an integral part of their lives, and even though she was not a musician, he fully understood why she loved the industry so much.

As she stood staring at her reflection in the mirror, she realized there was little she could do for her puffy eyes aside from slather on moisturizer and an extra coat of mascara, hoping her glasses would camouflage just how hung over she looked. Despite the late hour and a complete lack of coffee, she somehow managed to get to work on time, settling into her daily routine feeling sluggish but happy.

She wasn't sure which brought her more joy, knowing Micah seemed to not think of her in terms of her age, the fact they shared so many common interests, or the fact he was seriously kinky as fuck, just like her.

By lunch time she had already managed to get away from her desk twice to spend a few minutes messaging Micah, and each time her boss had had her paged over the intercom system because she wasn't sitting at her desk. It made her wonder what the fuck had happened to those supposed two fifteen-minute breaks they were entitled to each day. Feeling her blood pressure beginning to boil, Ember called Nicci a few minutes after twelve and asked her if she was ready to go grab a bite to eat before she went postal on someone. At the rate she was going, she would be completely grey-headed by five o'clock.

***

"Are you sure you're okay?" Nicci asked as she eyed Ember from across the table.

Ember looked up from her phone, absently taking another bite of her garden salad. "Yeah, I'm fine, why do you ask?"

Her friend shrugged. "You just seem quieter than usual. And you look like shit, to be honest. Are you not sleeping again, or did you get wasted and wake up in the laundry basket like last time?"

Ember nearly snorted, choking slightly on the bite of food in her mouth. *That's an understatement*, she thought to herself.

"If you are talking about sleep then no, I'm not sleeping as much as I would like, but it's not from the usual stresses. I'm good, actually," she added as she answered Micah's private message from within her Snapagram account. "And I only ended up in the laundry basket *once*, thank you very much."

Micah's Ember

She giggled as Micah sent her another snapshot of his naked ass, sprawled out on his bed.

Nicci stared at her friend, one eyebrow arched skyward. "Uh huh. What's his name?"

She looked up from her phone, her face blanching slightly before she suddenly blushed so fiercely the fiery red flush went clear up to her hairline. "What? No, it's not like that. I mean-" She stopped, at a loss for words.

"Damn, Ember, you act like I just accused you of raping someone, or robbing the cradle, or stealing something," she said with a laugh. But when her friend still sat there with her face as red as a beet, she couldn't help but feel a sudden twinge of nervousness. "Okay, girl, what the fuck is going on with you? You've been acting weird the past three weeks, even for you."

Ember took a swallow of her soda, not sure if she wanted anyone to know what she had been doing. It was weird enough she was carrying on a cyber relationship with someone, it was twice as sketchy considering he was literally young enough to be her son. But perhaps more concerning than anything, she was literally trusting him at his word when he said he was legal.

"Um, I don't think you really want to know anything about this, Nicci," she finally said, her words only fueling her friend's curiosity.

"Alright, girl, out with it. You know I won't judge you, no matter what. I've seen some of your photography, remember? Nothing wrong with admiring a nice ass, or getting involved with one."

Ember ducked her head, smiling sheepishly. "Okay, but really, I think the less specifics you know the better."

Her friend nodded. "Okay, deal. Just tell me, are you happy? Cause you seem to be glowing with

Micah's Ember

happiness, despite the whole being red-in-the-face thing, and looking like you slept on the bathroom floor."

The two of them laughed. "Yes, I'm happy. I can't say this is going anywhere relationship wise, but I'm having fun and it makes me happy. No one is getting hurt so, you know, no harm no foul, right?"

Nicci nodded her head. "So how old is he?" she asked point-blank, giving her friend a smirk.

Ember groaned. "Oh come on, what difference does it matter how old he is?"

"The only time a *woman* says something like that is when the guy is a whole hell of a lot younger than her. And like I said, I've seen your photography, so I know if you are "seeing" someone, and I use the term loosely, then it better damn well be someone younger, or else what's the point?"

The two of them giggled. "Okay, he's younger than me, like *a lot* younger, okay? He's legal, so don't get the wrong idea. He lives half-way across the country, he's a drummer for one of my fave bands, and it's just fun, you know? But he's really sweet, he's dead-fucking sexy, and I like chatting with him."

"Uh huh, I bet he's sexy," she said with a chuckle. "Wait, he isn't that drummer you were talking about earlier in the month, is he?"

Ember nodded. "Yeah. We've been chatting pretty much every day since then. Nothing serious, just having some fun together."

"Damn, Ember, leave it to you to rob the cradle."

"I'm not robbing the cradle," she replied, rolling her eyes despite the smile on her face. Just the thought of Micah's sexy ass sprawled across his bed made her weak in the knees and in serious

Micah's Ember

need of a dildo and about ten minutes of alone time.

"Just don't get hurt, okay? Guys that young are meant to be fun, but they aren't exactly relationship material."

"Relax, Nicci," Ember said, taking another bite of her salad. "We've been chatting for less than a month. It's not like we've made plans to move in together or anything."

"Hmm, if he's as sexy as you claim he is, I would probably have to send out a search party for you if the two of you ever got together."

They burst into laughter, their conversation turning easily to a new subject. In the back of her mind, though, Ember couldn't help but wonder what may lay ahead for the two of them as their weird relationship continued to develop via webcam and private messages. They may have only been chatting for a few weeks, but it already felt like she had known him half of her life.

Micah's Ember

Chapter 9

"Deeper, Ember, I want to hear you scream my name," Micah whispered eagerly as his hand worked his cock. His sleepy, aquamarine eyes watched her intently, his body on fire with desire.

"Micah, I want you so bad," she groaned, shoving her favorite glass dildo as far into her dripping center as she could, feeling the rounded tip bumping against her cervix.

Micah watched her through half-closed lids as she worked the dildo into her tight confines, loving the way she looked on her hands and knees in her skintight bodysuit, the little feather-tail of her butt-plug caressing her firm ass as she moved the smooth toy in and out of her soaked pussy faster and faster.

It was better than all the porn in the universe, made ten times hotter because he was the only one who got to watch her. He was the one who was making her cream herself, and it was *his* name she moaned every time she touched herself.

"I want you to come for me, Micah," she said, slowing down a bit so she could watch him.

"Yes ma'am," he groaned, his hips thrust upward as he whispered her name, the pearly droplets of cum shooting from the tip of his dick.

Ember licked her lips as she watched him, feeling her own release mount so quickly she

Micah's Ember

barely had time to do more than gasp before she was screaming his name, her own love juices squirting out of her, soaking the towel she had placed beneath her body.

She collapsed on her side, her dildo still shoved deep inside her. She moaned slightly, so exhausted she could barely move.

"Damn, woman, you are going to be the death of me. I'm not sure I could handle actually fucking you in person," he said with a chuckle.

"Why's that?" she asked, her eyes half-closed as she watched him.

"We'd both end up in the hospital I'm afraid. I'm not sure I'd ever be able to get enough of this. What does that make for you anyway, eight, nine times?"

She tried to shrug but couldn't muster the strength. "Eleven, actually, but who's counting?"

He groaned again. "What I wouldn't give to be there in person, my cock shoved deep inside of you instead of that damn toy of yours, to feel your pussy clench around my cock as you came."

"Mmm, no fair teasing. I'm so tired, but I'm still so fucking horny."

"*Still?*" he asked in surprise.

"Yeah, well, you're not the only one who wants that cock of yours shoved inside my pussy. This toy is nice, but I much prefer the real thing fucking me hard and fast until I pass out from exhaustion."

"Mmm, now who's teasing?"

They lay in comfortable silence for a few minutes, staring at each other through their cameras. "What time are ya'll leaving in the morning?" she finally asked, wishing like fuck they weren't going on tour so damn soon. The last few months had passed by so quickly, she could

Micah's Ember

scarcely believe it was time for them to go on tour already.

They had been "dating" for nearly three months now, spending every single night on camera with each other, fucking themselves senseless half the night and talking the other half. At this point they had talked about so much of their lives, their likes and dislikes, and any random idea which popped into their heads.

She had laughed so much in the past few months she felt like her face was stapled into a permanent smile. She wasn't getting more than four hours of sleep a night, but she wasn't complaining. If anything, she wished they had more time to talk. Going to work every day without access to their only mode of communication was practically torture for her.

He glanced at the clock on his nightstand. "Ugh, we're leaving in about two hours. I guess I need to get up and get a bath, make sure I got all my shit together."

She groaned, but she knew he was right. "I'm really going to miss our nightly chats," she whispered, still too tired to move. Saying the words out loud made her heart flutter rapidly inside her chest. She had to fight back the tears, the burning behind her eyes so fierce she was forced to blink a few times.

He smiled. "Me too. We're playing five, six nights a week, and we spend the nights in the van. I'm not sure how often I'll be able to get away from everyone for a quick chat."

"I know," she said with a sad smile. "You guys are going to be great. I expect lots of pics, and video if you guys can manage. At least give me *something* to hang on to until you get back home," she said with a chuckle.

"You know it. Do you have our tour schedule?"

Micah's Ember

She nodded. "Mmm hmm. And your driving route."

"Good," he said as continued to gaze sleepily at her. He seemed a bit down, as if he were feeling the same separation anxiety she was presently trying to get under control. "I'll try to let you know ahead of time when I can get a few minutes away. If nothing else, I'll call you, even if we can't get on cam."

She couldn't help but smile, even it were a bittersweet smile. "That would be really nice."

He sighed, once again eyeing the clock, trying hard to not let his disappointment show. His heart felt as if it were going to explode, or rip in two. It was an entirely new sensation, something he wasn't sure he was ready to accept. The thought of not getting to chat with her on a regular basis was nearly making him sick to his stomach with anxiety.

He sighed again, turning back to her. "I better go. If I'm late the guys will rag me for days." He tried to smile, but it looked more like a grimace as he felt his heart lurch inside of his chest once again at the thought of having to say goodbye for nearly four whole months. "I'll text you when we start on our way out, okay?"

"You better," she said, trying not to let the sadness seep in any more than it currently was. "Be careful," she whispered, feeling the tinge of tears burning brightly behind the backs of her eyes. She kept telling herself she was being silly, but she still couldn't help it. She felt like someone was trying to dig her heart out of her chest with a dull spoon.

"I will. Just wish you could make one of the shows."

She grinned. "Is that an invitation?"

Micah's Ember

"Hell yeah," he said with a chuckle. "Chat you soon, Em. I'll miss you."

"I'll miss you, too. Bye, Micah. Call me when you get a chance."

"You know it."

He hit the *disconnect* button on his Skipper account, blinking a few times as he wondered why his eyes were burning so badly.

Ember stared at her laptop screen for a few seconds, fighting back the tears. She kept telling herself she was being silly, but no matter how many times she repeated the words to herself, nothing could make the gnawing emptiness inside of her go away.

Micah's Ember

Chapter 10

The days began to flow into one another, each waking second of her regular job a larger thorn in her ass than she ever thought possible. She lived for the few text messages she received from Micah and the one or two times they managed to get a call into each other between her work schedule and his touring schedule. Sometimes it was two or three days before he could manage to get away from everyone long enough to give her a quick call.

For now, she lived off of the daily texts he sent to her early in the morning before she had to be at work. Sometimes he managed to get a quick call in prior to midnight, while he was waiting on the rest of the band to get ready to meet their fans after a show. It wasn't much, but it was something, and she treasured those few moments of finally hearing his sweet voice more than her next breath.

In the past two-and-a-half months they had only managed to get on their Skipper accounts with each other twice, and it was for less than half-an-hour each time, leaving both of them incredibly frustrated and missing each other more than they already did. They both knew they wouldn't be able to satisfy their desires with him being on the road with his band mates right up under him at all times, but it was still a very bitter pill to swallow

Micah's Ember

when they did manage to get a few minutes of camera time.

As the clock continued to move forward, Ember felt as if she were going to lose her mind if she didn't get to spend some actual time with him. Their relationship had barely begun five months ago, but she felt as if she had known him for years. She no longer even thought about the age difference between them; he was just Micah, someone she had grown very fond of during their nightly encounters together.

Ember had spent a solid week checking the band's driving routes and all of their shows. There were exactly three shows which were close enough to be considered within driving distance from her. After rearranging her work schedule and taking a few days off, she soon discovered herself with the trunk of her car packed with enough clothes and supplies for an entire week spent following the band around on tour. Of course, that is, *if* Micah didn't freak out when he actually met her.

On Sunday shortly before noon, just shy of twenty-two weeks after this whole crazy cyber BDSM relationship started, Ember finally hit the road, intent upon driving the six hours to Pensacola where she had every intention of spending the next six days following *Tempered Souls* around while they toured in Florida, Georgia, and Alabama. She had already purchased tickets to the five shows they had scheduled to play, and she wasn't sure if she was more excited or nervous about it. Literally *anything* could happen during this next week, be it good or bad.

Feeling her heart skip a beat, Ember steadied her nerves, praying she wasn't about to make one of the largest mistakes of her life.

***

Micah's Ember

It was nearly six in the afternoon, just three hours until *Tempered Souls* was scheduled to take the stage at a small bar in Pensacola. Ember pulled up to the tiny motel on the outskirts of town, hoping the inside was more inviting than the outside. Thankfully the room was clean and well-kept, at least to the naked eye. Not wanting to take any chances though, she quickly stripped down the bed and immediately sprayed it with pesticide and then covered it with a thick, plastic sheet before pulling out the bedclothes she had packed with her. The last thing she wanted while on this trip was to bring home God-only-knew-what from the few dingy hotels she had booked.

Feeling satisfied she wouldn't end up with some exotic pest nestled next to her while she slept, she brought in one of her small overnight bags and took a shower. She then spent the next hour mentally going through all the outfits she had brought with her.

She had spent nearly two weeks systematically putting together everything she planned to wear on this trip, from her fetish outfits right down to which set of underwear she would wear under what outfit and at which show. She felt like she had OCD before she had managed to hammer out the details of her wardrobe. She was looking for *any* excuse which would take her mind off the fact she was secretly going to surprise the barely-legal man she had been cyber-sexing with for nearly half a year.

At quarter 'til eight, Ember finally managed to talk herself into getting into her car and driving the half-hour to the venue. As she parked her car and weaved her way through the crowd, she had never been so nervous in her life. She wasn't quite sure how well Micah would take to her suddenly

Micah's Ember

showing up at one of his shows, much less the fact she planned to follow the band around for an entire week.

As far she knew, the rest of the band wasn't even aware of their relationship. She could just imagine how all of this was going to appear to them. And that wasn't even counting whether or not they would actually get along once they met. She didn't even want to think about the possibility he may be so turned off once he actually met her she ended up having to go straight home the next day.

Every few seconds she glanced at her phone. Micah had texted her earlier stating he would have a few minutes before the show to call her via Skipper. Her already out-of-control heart felt like it was cutting cartwheels inside of her chest while her stomach rumbled around like she had swallowed a dozen squirming earthworms. If she didn't already feel like she was about to crawl right out of her skin, she might have been concerned.

Her phone suddenly began vibrating in her hand. She looked down, seeing her Skipper app announcing an incoming call from Micah. Her heart leaped into her throat as her stomach tied itself into a double-knot. She had to swallow down the sudden surge of nausea which swept through her body.

"*Fuck me running, it's now or never,*" she muttered to herself. She took a deep breath, plastered a smile on her face and hit the *accept* button on the app.

"Hey!" she said, hoping her voice didn't sound as high-pitched and squeaky to him as it did to her.

"Hey yourself," he said, his brow furrowing at all of the background noise. "What are you doing?" he asked, unconsciously raising his voice.

Micah's Ember

"Um, well, funny story," she said, the sight of his face instantly calming her. "I kinda decided to go see this band I've been wanting to see for about a year now. I have this huge crush on their drummer, and, well … maybe you know the band?" She turned slightly so her back was to the stage, allowing him to see the huge *Tempered Souls* banner which was stretched across the stage.

His beautiful aquamarine eyes grew wide in his face as his mouth fell open slightly. She watched as he visible swallowed. "Ember, are you telling me you are currently in Pensacola inside the same bar I am?"

"Um, it depends on how pissed you are that I showed up unannounced," she said, her face flushing a bit as she unconsciously fluffed the back of her pixie-like haircut. She looked back at her phone, seeing the camera feed on Micah's end swirling crazily.

"Micah? What are you doing?" she asked as she felt the nervousness settle into the pit of her stomach all over again. The worms which had been previously housed there suddenly morphed into butterflies, making her feel like she was going to barf all over the floor. "Micah?" she asked worriedly.

A solid minute passed by and the feed on his end was still spinning around like his phone had been tossed inside a clothes dryer. Someone to the far right of her screamed, causing her to turn around as she craned her neck trying to see what was going on. A few seconds later Micah walked out onto the stage, yelling her name as he scanned the crowd.

Ember felt her heart flip over inside of her again, the sight of him in the flesh making her want to scream and faint all at the same time. Her heart lurched before smashing itself against her rib

Micah's Ember

cage where it began beating like a crazed, trapped beast. She felt light headed and fuzzy-brained, the desire to throw herself at him and start crying mixed in with a scorching heat which zinged straight through her. She could only imagine this must be what Beatle Mania had been like.

She discovered herself smiling like an idiot as she lifted her arms above her head and began waving them around, screaming his name in an attempt to be heard over the crowd. Not being tall enough to be seen over the people around her, she started jumping up and down, flailing about like a woman gone insane.

Micah could hear her, but it took a few seconds to pick her out of the crowd. He felt both a rush of relief surge through his body as well as his heart fluttering violently inside his chest as he looked at her. Without thinking he rushed to the edge of the makeshift stage, a huge smile on his face as reached out to help her onto the stage. As she finally stood there in front of him, he was awe-struck at just how beautiful she was – and at just how tiny she was in person. They both could feel their hearts hammering away inside their chests, the sound of the blood rushing through their veins drowning out the heavy noise of so many people packed inside the small bar.

They stood staring at each for a brief second, their eyes roaming over each other's body before Micah swooped her up into his arms, swirling her around as she laughed. Suddenly all of her apprehension, her fears, and her doubts disappeared as she finally fell into his warm embrace.

After a few seconds Micah set her back on her feet, his eyes boring into hers, both of them oblivious to the fact they were standing on a stage inside a packed nightclub with hundreds of eyes

Micah's Ember

watching them. A lot of the people at the front of the stage were whispering and taking photos, but neither of them seemed to notice.

He reached up, tucking a stray piece of strawberry blonde hair behind her ear. "I've missed you," he whispered.

Ember felt her heart swell at his sentiment, the terror she had been feeling just a half-hour earlier washed away with those three simple words. She was once again smiling, that stupid grin spread across her face as the past two months spent without him was quickly forgotten like a bad dream.

"I've missed you, too," she replied as he took her hand and pulled her off stage.

No sooner than the two of them were away from prying eyes than he backed her into a corner, his lips capturing hers in a brutal kiss. It was everything she had imagined it would be, and more. Her lips yielded to his, her mouth opening to allow his tongue access, a small moan escaping her as she wrapped her arms around his neck. His lips were just as delicious as she imagined they would be, soft and warm, gentle yet demanding. The entire world around them disappeared as he kissed her, her body pressed eagerly against his.

"Damn, Ember, you taste so good," he said breathlessly as she shoved her hands underneath his shirt.

"Remember what I said I wanted to do to you backstage, if I ever got the chance?" she asked as she looked at him, her blue eyes twinkling in the low light.

He slowly nodded his head, his dick already so hard it ached. He had barely laid eyes on her before his desire to touch and taste her had taken hold, his body on fire to finally feel himself buried

Micah's Ember

balls-deep inside the tempting honey pot he had only had the pleasure of seeing on camera.

"Tell me what you want, Micah," she whispered as she trailed her nails slowly down his abdomen. She was so horny her entire center ached, and she could already feel her love juices making her bodysuit slick with her desire.

He hissed as he wrapped his arm around her waist. "I want to fuck you, Ember, I want to finally feel my cock buried deep inside that little pussy of yours," he said hoarsely. Nothing else mattered, only finally feeling her body against his, to feel himself inside her just as he had imagined for weeks on end.

Her entire body jerked at his words, the look of desire in his eyes driving her crazy with her own lust. She lifted the short, ruffled skirt she wore, showing him the same red latex bodysuit she had worn on camera for him many times in the past few months.

"*Fuck me*, you damn little tease," he groaned, reaching down to unzip the 'easy-access' panel in the crotch of the suit, wasting no time in plunging his fingers deep inside of her already soaked pussy.

"Micah," she said as she moaned deep in her throat, gasping as his fingers finally found their way inside of her, a sensation she had been dreaming about for so long she had thought she would go mad from her own lustful fantasies. Nothing compared to the sensation of finally feeling his body pressed against hers, his fingers buried deep inside her. As much as she had dreamed and fantasized about this moment, as much as she had imagined how it would be, nothing compared to the real thing.

She kissed him again, her mouth hot and demanding as her hips moved in small circles as

Micah's Ember

he moved his finger slowly in and out of her dripping center. Her entire body was on fire, like someone had doused her nerve endings in gasoline. She wanted him more than she wanted her next breath, needed to feel him inside of her. It was all consuming, her body making so many demands it left her mind completely oblivious to anything and everything else.

"Micah, *please*," she gasped as her hands moved to quickly unbutton his jeans. "I want to feel you inside of me. Please, you are driving me insane!"

He groaned, removing his fingers and picking her up so she could wrap her legs around his waist as he pulled his stiff cock out of his pants.

She didn't want gentle, had no time for foreplay. Just as soon as she felt the tip of his dick at her entrance, she plunged herself downward, impaling herself on his massive cock. He gasped, the feeling of himself suddenly buried balls-deep inside of her hot, wet cavern almost too delicious to comprehend. No amount of fantasizing could have possibly prepared him for just how wonderfully tight she felt.

"Yes," she said as she groaned again, using her legs as leverage as she quickly lifted herself up only to impale herself again, over and over, riding him like her own personal fuck toy.

"*Fuck yes*," he hissed, the sensation of his cock wrapped inside her hot flesh causing the tingling inside of his balls to rise up faster than he ever thought possible. He couldn't ever remember being this turned on before in his entire life, not even as a teenager.

He held her captive against the wall as he drove himself into her, hard, fast, not giving her any time to get used to his considerable girth. She moaned each time he thrust upward, his cock

Micah's Ember

bottoming out inside of her tight confines over and over again. Within just a few short minutes they were both gasping each other's name, feeling themselves crashing over the edge of into oblivion, completely engulfed in the sensation of their shared lust for each other.

As the two of them slowly came out of their lust-filled haze, Micah reluctantly withdrew his still-hard cock from within her. She wasted no time in zipping the 'easy-access' panel closed, loving the way his cum seeped out of her to coat the inside of the suit. She gasped at the sensation, forcing herself to resist the urge to dry-hump his leg. The thought of how it would feel to rub her pussy against the inside of her suit made slick by their combined love juices was almost enough to make her come all over again.

He bent down and reclaimed her lips with his, unwilling to let her go just yet. His phone had been buzzing in his back pocket for the last two minutes straight, a painful reminder he had a show to perform.

"How long are you staying?" he finally asked, reluctantly releasing her lips.

She sighed, a happy smile on her face. "Depends. I've got a week off of work and my car packed full of shit. If you don't mind me tagging along, I've got tickets for every show this week."

He blinked at her for a second before a huge grin spread across his face. "Seriously?"

She returned his lop-sided smile, her head tilted to the side as she stared at him with her big, blue eyes. "Yeah, that is, if you want me hanging around that long."

"Oh fuck yes, why would you even think I didn't want you around?" he asked as he laughed, picking her up and kissing her hard on the mouth.

Micah's Ember

His phone began vibrating inside his back pocket again, causing both of them to laugh. "Fuck, I better get back to the rest of the guys before Spence sends out a search party."

She grinned at him, her hand cupping the side of his face as her eyes drank in the sight of him. "Guess I better go grab a good seat then."

He nodded. "See you after our set?"

"You know it," she replied as he reluctantly released her, the two of them glancing back at each other as they went their separate ways.

Micah's Ember

Chapter 11

It had taken Micah nearly three solid hours after the show to get through the crowd of fans and well-wishers. For Ember, it felt like an eternity. As much as she loved sitting back and watching as the young fan-girls rubbed their tight bodies against Micah, her own body was making major demands of its own. All she wanted was to finally have him stripped naked and laying in her bed, to be all hers if just for a few hours of unbridled, lustful fun.

They had never discussed their relationship, so it came as no surprise when the rest of the band just blinked at Micah when he introduced her as just "Ember." The name meant nothing to them, as she figured it wouldn't. They seemed mildly surprised he was hanging around someone who seemed more than a few years his senior, but they didn't question him about it.

She wasn't quite sure if she should be insulted or happy about his continued vagueness concerning their relationship to each other. On the one hand, she couldn't imagine his band mates would be as open-minded to their relationship as he was, and she sincerely doubted it would help his image in the rock scene. Rock stars tended to have a much more successful career when they were unattached and available. On the other hand,

Micah's Ember

however, the woman in her couldn't help but feel insecure, wondering if he was ashamed of her or their relationship.

In the beginning, he seemed oddly embarrassed by the attention he was receiving from his young female fans. He periodically glanced at Ember, but she just smiled at him and nodded her head, giving him permission to enjoy himself and bask in all the occasional crotch-grabbing and dry-humping going on by some of his more zealous fans. He was young, he was hot as fuck, and until they agreed to cement their "relationship" on a more permanent basis, she didn't see any reason why he shouldn't enjoy the perks of being a hot, young rocker.

His slightly flushing face soon gave way to big smiles as he peeked at Ember every so often, making lude gestures and generally enjoying himself. Ember just sat back and watched, knowing by the end of the night he was going to end up in her bed, screaming *her* name, with all the little fan-girls long forgotten. Watching him getting his ass grabbed and the girls trying their best to kiss him was a small price to pay to have him in her life.

As the bar called for last rounds, Micah finally excused himself from the rest of the band, edging his way closer to the door where Ember was patiently waiting for him. Just as the two of them caught up with each other and were preparing to leave, Spence materialized out of nowhere, causing a ripple of concern to radiate through her body.

"Hey, Micah, where are you off to in such a hurry? We got to get everything loaded into the van. We'll be hitting the road in a few hours."

Micah gave him a sheepish grin, dodging a glance at Ember. "Yeah, can you guys make it without me? I've been promising Ember we'd get

Micah's Ember

caught up for months now. She drove out of state to see me and I'd really like to spend some time with her before we hit the road."

Spence eyed Ember, his dark brown eyes actually looking at her for the first time. He took in her short skirt, ragged tee-shirt, and high-heels, his eyebrow raising slightly as he began to wonder who she *really* was. "Um, yeah, okay. We can manage for one night. How long you going to be gone?"

He shrugged. "Can't really say. Why don't I just meet you at that gas station right up the road at around five? You guys won't have to wait up for me."

Spence once again looked over at Ember as if he were sizing her up, his brain trying to figure out how she fit into Micah's life. "Sure. Who did you say you were again? Micah's aunt, or cousin or something?"

Ember raised one slightly arched eyebrow, her blue eyes darting over to Micah. She wasn't even remotely sure how to answer that one, so she opted to keep silent. Since even *she* wasn't really sure what was going on between them, she hardly knew what to say.

"Ugh, Spence, we've got to go. It's getting late and I don't want to waste what little bit of time we have left before we hit the road again. I've got my phone, if you need me call or text. I'll see you guys in a few hours."

Spence just nodded his head and mumbled, "Okay."

Micah put his hand around Ember's waist, quickly ushering her out the door before his band mate could start asking more questions he was unwilling to answer right now.

Spence watched them through narrowed eyes as they left the bar. Micah had been acting strange

Micah's Ember

the past few months. He was ditching practice, using all kinds of weird excuses for running late for rehearsals. Then there was the few times he had interrupted Micah while he was chatting with someone on the phone.

More concerning to Spence was Micah's sudden secretive behavior. Normally his drummer was practically an open book, always in a good mood and more than happy to sit around and chat for hours. But over the past few months he was spending less and less time with the band, offering up strange excuses for his behavior, and slowly withdrawing from the rest of them. He was still happy, still smiling, but the usual chatty drummer had slowly stopped sharing a huge chunk of his life with them.

Spence shook his head as he watched the two of them walk out the door together, Micah smiling and laughing as they exited the building. Exactly who was this woman, and how did she fit into his drummer's life?

***

Micah and Ember had barely made it out of her car before they were wrapped in each other's arms, their mouths hot and demanding as their tongues wrestled with each other. Ember somehow managed to get the door open, the two of them falling inside and onto the bed within seconds.

Ember had packed a little suitcase filled with some of the new toys and gadgets she had purchased over the course of their cyber-relationship, but she had not brought any of it inside the hotel with her. She had been so unsure of how her presence would be received, she had decided against bringing it in until she knew how Micah would react. Now, as they ripped each

Micah's Ember

other's clothes off in their haste to feel each other's naked flesh, trying out that new vibrating dildo was the furthest thing from her mind. All she wanted at that moment in time was to have his cock buried inside of her.

"Micah," she groaned as she finally had him sprawled out on her bed, her eyes feasting on the sight of his naked body. "You are absolutely gorgeous," she whispered, bending down to kiss him on the lips again.

Their tongues danced with each other, twirling and tasting, his full lips causing her to go weak in the knees. But she wanted to taste all of him, so she released his lips, causing him to moan slightly in disappointment.

Her mouth trailed a line of fiery kisses down his body, each touch of her mouth igniting a fresh new blaze of desire within him. Her teeth teased and nibbled at his flesh as she kissed her way inch by delicious inch down his chest. She loved how he gasped, his back arching slightly as her teeth grazed his stomach, his hands wrapped in her hair.

She wiggled her way in between his thighs, gazing up at him through her lashes as she took his dick in her hand, resisting the urge to shove all of him into her mouth at once. Instead, she teased his cockhead with her tongue, running slow circles around the tip until she finally popped it into her eager mouth. She moved her mouth down on him a few centimeters at a time before moving back up, each new downward stroke taking more and more of him into her eager mouth, a tantalizing dance which soon had him groaning and thrusting his hips as he tried desperately to cram himself into her throat.

Finally, she had worked all of him as deep into her waiting mouth as she could possibly get him,

Micah's Ember

her hands working at his shaft as she bobbed her head up and down, each new stroke slightly faster than the last. She kept at this for a few minutes until he was panting heavily as he wiggled on the bed.

"Em, you keep that up and I'm going to come."

She giggled slightly, the vibration causing him to squeal as the pleasure coursed through his body to settle at the base of his dick. He hissed, his hips thrust upward as she slowly removed her mouth.

"Mmm, not yet you don't," she said with a smile, moving to straddle his hard cock. She slid him inside of her, slow at first, but as soon as she felt his cockhead inside of her, she wasted no time in impaling herself on the object of her desire.

The two of them groaned in unison as he bottomed out inside of her, the feeling of him filling her up so completely one of the most wondrous sensations she had ever felt. Within a few minutes they had worked up a fast rhythm, the two of them fucking each other harder and faster with each thrust. She ground herself against him, feeling his dickhead hitting the back of her cervix with every upward plunge of his cock. She had never had her pussy crammed so full in her life, and she absolutely loved it.

"Fuck, Micah, you feel so damn good," she moaned, grinding her pubic bone into his, feeling herself just before spilling over the edge of another orgasm.

"Yes, harder, please, fuck me harder," she purred as he held onto her waist, shoving himself impossibly deep, the tingling in his balls growing until he finally erupted inside of her.

She screamed slightly as rammed himself to the hilt inside of her, her slick cavern clenching around his dick as she spilt over the edge, her inner muscles tightening around his cock again

Micah's Ember

and again until they both finally collapsed, exhausted and only mildly content.

The two of them lay together, his dick still shoved deep inside of her as their limbs were entwined, their breathing slowly returning to normal.

"Holy fuck, that was beyond amazing," she whispered. She propped herself up on her elbow so she could gaze at him, her fingers lightly tracing the outline of his lips.

His tongue darted out, licking her fingers before he popped them into his mouth, sucking on them gently. She groaned, the feel of his still hard cock inside of her aching center making the lust rise up inside of her again.

"Keep doing that and I'll be dry humping your leg in just a few minutes," she said with throaty chuckle.

He grinned at her. "Why dry hump when you can just ride me again?" he asked, his eyes twinkling in the dim light of the room.

A slow smile spread across her face. "Round two?"

He nodded his head, his eyes watching her as she leaned down to kiss him. His hands held her waist captive as he slowly thrust his still hard cock into her, their desire for each other quickly burning out of control all over again.

***

An insistent ringing roused them from a contented, sex-induced slumber. Micah fumbled around in the dark, his hand finally grasping his phone where it lay on the nightstand. His eyes stared blankly at his phone for a second before the sleep-induced haze finally lifted. As his brain

Micah's Ember

registered the time, he bolted out of the bed, letting out a little yelp.

"Oh shit, I'm late!" he yelled as he staggered around, trying to find his underwear in the early morning light streaming through the threadbare curtains.

Ember hopped out of bed, the two of them darting around frantically as they got dressed. She could just imagine what she must look like, her hair sticking up all over her head and half her makeup smeared off her face. She would have laughed had they both not fallen asleep, ensuring the entire band would no doubt be late getting back on the road.

Within a few minutes they were back in her car, heading toward the gas station as Micah called Spence back, letting him know they would be there in half an hour.

She hit the interstate, speeding toward the rendezvous which would take Micah back to his band mates, and away from her until that night. She tried not to think about it, not wanting the happiness she had felt for the past ten hours to be replaced by the gnawing ache she felt each time she thought about having to leave him.

"You have tickets for tonight's show, right?" he asked as they sped down the highway, her speedometer inching its way closer to ninety miles an hour.

"Yes. Show starts at eight?"

He nodded.

"Do I need to meet you before the show starts?" she asked a bit timidly, still unsure of exactly how much information he was willing to tell his friends when it came to their relationship.

"Definitely. I'm not really sure what the rest of the guys have planned once we get to Huntsville. I can text you once I talk to them," he said, rubbing

Micah's Ember

the back of his head. "It's kinda hard to make plans when you are riding with a bunch of other people."

She smiled. "Yeah, I know. Just keep in mind I'm driving as well so if you ever want to hitch a ride with me during the week, just let me know, okay?" As soon as the words were out of her mouth, she wondered if maybe she was being too forward, even a bit pushy. If Micah planned on keeping the nature of their "relationship" a secret from the rest of the band, spending more time with her might not even be possible.

"Sure. I'll find out what's on the menu for today and let you know," he said as they pulled into the gas station, the band's van sitting in the far corner of the parking lot, looking very much out of place as a half-dozen eighteen wheelers pulled in to fuel up for the day.

She pulled in next to them, leaving the car running as Micah opened the door. She wanted to kiss him, to ask him to ride with her instead, to tell him she would miss him, but she didn't. Instead she smiled at him as he got out of the car, leaning down to tell her quickly, "I'll call you," before he closed the door. She nodded even though he was already at the van, laughing with his band mates as they all loaded up to head down the road.

He looked back at her as he got into the van, waving at her as he gave her another one of those beautiful smiles.

She felt her heart lurch inside her chest, an odd mixture of bitter-sweet sadness washing over her as she watched him leave.

Micah's Ember

Chapter 12

"Where the fuck you been all night man?" Nik, their bassist, asked as Micah settled into the back of the van.

"I was catching up with Ember," he replied, avoiding Nik's dark brown gaze as he fumbled with his earphones. He could feel his cheeks already flushing, but he tried to hide it. There was no way he wanted any of them sticking their noses into his private life, at least when it came to Ember and their relationship.

"Who the fuck is Ember?" Nik asked.

"You spent the whole night with that chick?" Spence asked, eyeing Micah through the review mirror. He was frowning, but all Micah could see was his eyes.

Nik leaned over and sniffed Micah's shirt, jerking back dramatically as he waved his hand in front of his face, his nose crinkling. "Dude! You reek of sweat, sex, and shame!"

Micah turned around in his seat and swatted at Nik's shoulder. "I do *not* smell like shame!"

Their guitarist, Zachery, had been sitting quietly in the front seat. Suddenly he turned around to stare at the two of them. "What the hell did I miss last night?"

"I love how he didn't protest to smelling like sex, only the shame part!" Nik said with a laugh, pulling back before Micah could land another punch on his shoulder.

"Man, don't tell me you *slept* with that old chick," Spence said, sitting up straighter in his seat so he could glare at his drummer through the mirror. His brown eyes narrowed as he stared at Micah.

"Who the fuck is Ember and why is Micah fucking her?" Zachery demanded, glancing between Spence's disgusted face and Micah's pink cheeks. Man, he really *had* missed a lot of last night's action from the look of it.

"Dude, she's like old enough to be your mom or some shit, Micah," Spence said, the obvious revulsion evident in his voice. "I know you like kink but *fuck* man, why you out screwing the grandmas?"

Micah's slightly blushing face suddenly flushed red with anger. "She is *not* old enough to be my mom, you jackass. The only reason why you even know she's older than me is because I told you. And even if I *were* screwing her, it's hardly anyone's business." He glared at Spence's reflection in the mirror, his lips drawn down in anger.

"Damn, man, don't get you panties all in a bunch. If you would rather go fuck the cougars than the hot, young things at our shows, you go right ahead, no skin off my nose," Spence muttered, dropping the subject.

"Who the fuck is Ember?" Zachery asked again.

Nik looked over at him, shaking his head.

"*Drop it*," Micah said, his voice low in his anger.

Zachery ducked his head, squirming around in his seat. He'd never seen Micah be anything but happy-go-lucky in the two years he had been with

Micah's Ember

the band. He had always thought of him as a big, happy teddy bear, always smiling, always happy, and never a cross word said to anyone. Seeing his face flushed with anger and the warning in his voice sent a chill down his spine.

"Fine, whatever," Zachery mumbled as he turned back around in his seat, his dark brown eyes gazing absently out the window.

Micah settled back in his seat, his arms crossed across his chest. He had never felt this angry before, about anything, much less a woman. Hell, he hadn't even gotten that angry when his girlfriend of nearly two years refused to move to Michigan with him when he joined *Tempered Souls*.

He didn't know why it bothered him so much what the rest of the band thought of Ember. He was the one dating her, or whatever the hell they were doing. It shouldn't matter to them one way or the other what type of relationship he was in or with whom. Still, Spence's calloused remarks about her age really pissed him off. It made him acutely aware of just what type of whispers he would encounter if he continued with this relationship. Her age seemed like such a trivial thing to him now, and it really pissed him off to think everyone, including his band mates, would form an opinion about her based on that one inconsequential thing without even bothering to get to know her.

Feeling an uneasiness settle in the pit of his stomach, Micah hit *play* on his music app as he leaned back and closed his eyes. He needed some sleep, but when it finally came to claim him, his dreams were filled with bright blue eyes and a musical laugh which made his heart beat faster and slower, all at the same time.

***

Micah's Ember

Ember drove straight through to their next gig, stopping just long enough to gas up her car and grab a quick bite to eat before hitting the road again. It was barely noon when she arrived in Huntsville, giving her another five hours before she could check into her hotel. Feeling tired and oddly depressed, she pulled into a small gas station to freshen up and check out the sights and activities offered by the city. She checked her phone every few minutes, waiting for a text or call from Micah which never came.

An hour later, with nothing left to do and still no word from Micah, she decided to drive to a nearby strip mall and do some window shopping. What she really wanted to do was take a much-needed nap, but she was afraid to try to sleep in her car for fear of getting a ticket or something equally as cringe-worthy. At this point she had slept barely an hour since leaving her house on Sunday.

At around three, she caved and sent Micah a text, asking where they were and if he wanted to meet up before the show. The last thing she wanted to do was come off as a clingy, overly needy woman, but at the same time, she *had* driven out of state to finally meet him. The least he could do was text her and let her know what was going on, even if it was nothing more than a quick *going to sleep, chat you later* text.

Exhausted, she drove to her hotel and managed to sweet-talk the receptionist into letting her check in early. She took a bath and curled up in the bed, thankful to finally be able to lay down for a while. She drifted off to sleep almost immediately, one hand still wrapped around her phone as she waited for some word from Micah.

Micah's Ember

***

The insistent buzzing of her phone's alarm slowly roused her from a troubled sleep. She looked at the clock, rubbing her eyes as she tried to focus on the display. It was nearly five in the evening, giving her just shy of two hours to get ready and get to the venue. She was so tired, she wondered if she would come out better if she stayed and slept that extra hour. As soon as the thought crossed her mind, she immediately dismissed it, her body eager to see Micah again.

As she sat up on the bed, she flipped through her messages, feeling her heart sink a little when there was still nothing from Micah. She couldn't help but notice her phone noted the fact he had opened the message, but he had not bothered to reply to it. She could only hope it was because he didn't know what they had planned aside from the show. Sighing, she got up and went to get ready, wondering if she should even bother wearing the sexy negligee she had picked out or not.

Ember got dressed quickly, putting on a smidge of makeup and fixing her pixie-style hair before heading out the door. It was still an hour before the doors to the venue even opened, and two hours before *Tempered Souls* was scheduled to hit the stage. With nothing else to do, she decided to just drive to the venue and wait for the doors to open, hoping Micah wouldn't mind her presence. It wasn't like he didn't know she was going to be at all of his shows this week. Still, his continued silence was more than a bit concerning.

As she got into her car, her phone began ringing, her heart flip-flopping inside her chest slightly as she saw Micah's name appear on the screen. Taking a deep breath, she swiped the *accept* button and said a cheerful, "Hey, stranger!"

Micah's Ember

He paused, feeling his own heart lurch inside of his chest as soon as he heard her. He hadn't realized how much he had missed her voice, her smile, and it made him wonder why he hadn't called her earlier.

"Hey, Ember! Sorry, I know I was supposed to have called, but we ran into a bit of a snag today and we've been trying to fix it pretty much all day."

Her brow furrowed. "Snag? What kind of snag?" she asked, her stomach immediately clenching up in concern as she unconsciously bit her bottom lip.

"Well, kind of a funny story. The van broke down, *again*. One of the bands playing tonight came to get our stuff, but they didn't have enough room for all of us. Plus someone had to stay to get the van towed and put in the shop to be fixed."

"Okay. So are they coming back to get you guys?"

"That's the thing. We're nearly an hour out from the venue and the guys just left with our stuff. By the time they got everything unloaded and drove back, they would have missed their set as well as ours."

She smiled. "Micah, do I need to come pick you guys up and take you to the venue?"

He felt his heart lurch at the thought of having the others spend nearly an hour in the same car with her. As much as he loved the idea of spending more time with her, just the way Spence had acted when he just *thought* he had hooked up with Ember was enough to turn his stomach.

He had really hoped the rest of the band would be willing to get to know her, but from the way Spence acted, he thought it might not be such a good idea. He honestly didn't know where Spence's dislike of her was coming from, or why he even disliked her in the first place. Spence seemed more

Micah's Ember

concerned with their age difference than anything else, or at least that's the way he came off to Micah.

"Actually, it's just me, but yeah, I do need a ride. Hope you don't mind. I know I've been kinda ignoring you today, but we've been stuck in the outskirts of Decatur half the day. We thought we were going to be able to get the van fixed today and back on the road, but the shop we had it towed to took four hours to tell us they didn't have the parts needed and would have to have them overnighted to even get the thing fixed by tomorrow afternoon."

He sighed. He had been in a foul mood ever since Spence had given him the third degree this morning. His temperament had been made worse by the snide comments his band mates had been making about Ember, her age, and their relationship. Now, just hearing Ember's voice again made him wonder why he had been avoiding her all day, or why even cared what his band mates, or anyone else for that matter, thought about her and their relationship.

"No, it's okay. I get it, you guys have stuff to do and this is the last thing you need to deal with. I was actually just on my way to the venue, so I'll drive down and grab you," she said as she turned the key over in the ignition of her car. "I think I'm about forty-five minutes out from Decatur. Where are you exactly?"

He told her the name of the mechanic shop he was at, giving her a few minutes while she set her GPS and pulled out onto the highway. Soon she was cruising down the road, the two of them easily slipping back into their usual conversations as if nothing had happened.

***

Micah's Ember

Ember managed to get Micah back to the venue within a half-hour of their set time. He kissed her quickly before leaving, turning around and giving her a huge grin as he waved. She felt the searing heat scorch its way to her groin yet again, making her want to follow him backstage and screw him right and proper before his set. She knew they didn't have the time, and honestly she would really like to be able to fuck him without being in a hurry. Unfortunately, between the drive times and them spending so much time after each set to hang with their fans, there wasn't a whole lot of time left for them to spend together.

It sucked, but it just went with dating, or in her case screwing, a member of the band. At this point, she was just thankful she was able to spend any time with him at all. After so many months of watching him on camera, finally having him in the flesh was at least a step in the right direction.

Feeling an odd mix of jealousy, pride, and sadness, Ember made her way to the front of the stage, enjoying the music of *Five Days Gone* while she waited for Micah and the rest of the band to hit the stage.

***

"So how are ya'll getting to your next set?"

Ember glanced over at the young, fake blonde sitting between Micah and Zachery, her overly made-up eyes looking odd in her small face. The girl glanced back and forth between the two of them, smiling and giggling every few seconds.

She resisted the urge to roll her eyes. The girl, Tammy if her memory served correctly, had been flirting with the entire band. She had initially set her sights on Micah, but he had shot her down cold. Now she had taken to touching their arms,

Micah's Ember

"accidentally" brushing her large tits against their shoulders, and laughing at literally *everything* any single one of them said. It was enough to make her gag. It also made her wonder if she had been that addle-brained when she had been that age.

Tammy had taken one look at Ember sitting so close to Micah and asked her if she was his mom. Both her and Micah had laughed, him putting his arm around Ember's waist and pulling her tightly against him, giving Tammy a lop-sided grin.

The girl's eyes had grown wide, but she didn't say anything. Of course, Micah still was only introducing her as "Ember." Not as his girlfriend, not as a friend, just "Ember." Whether he liked the shock factor of letting everyone think he was dating her, or if he was just using her as an excuse to not have to get too friendly with the natives, she wasn't quite sure.

In all honestly, she wasn't sure if she should be grateful or pissed. On the one hand, she was a bit insulted, but on the other hand, exactly what *were* they to each other? They weren't officially "dating," and heaven only knew what kind of shit storm would start up if they actually did start seeing each other exclusively. For now, the band just assumed she was another cougar out screwing a pretty boy, and Micah was more than happy to let them think it. He kept his distance from all the touchy-feely little fan-girls, keeping her close even if he wasn't acknowledging their relationship with each other. She guessed it beat him introducing her as his "fuckbuddy." She supposed she should be thankful for small favors.

Ember looked over at Tammy, waiting for someone to answer her. She had been wondering the same thing, but hadn't had the guts to ask Micah about it yet. She half-hoped the rest of the band would just hitch a ride with *Five Days Gone*

Micah's Ember

and leave Micah behind to ride to the next venue with her. Unfortunately, someone would have to stay behind and drive the van, and there was little reason to split the band up three ways. Too much could happen, and the last thing they needed was to end up missing a show because she wanted to spend more time with her barely legal lover.

Spence shrugged. "We actually haven't thought that far ahead," he said with a laugh before he knocked back another long swallow of his beer.

The rest of the guys joined in, but it made Ember uneasy. Maybe she was just too damn old to be living on a wing and a prayer. The thought of being stuck in some unknown town with little resources and no family made her sick to her stomach with worry. How were they going to pay for things, eat, make it to their next show?

Of course, she also wasn't surrounded by a few hundred fans who were more than willing to do whatever it took to make sure they made it to their next gig. While the thought of being pretty much broke out on the road made her cringe, when you had fans to fall back on, other band mates, and lots of experience, she guessed it wasn't nearly as nerve-racking for them as it was for her.

"I guess we'll find out how bad the damage is tomorrow and go from there," Spence said as he picked up his beer and drained the glass.

Ember leaned over toward Micah, her voice low as she asked, "So what happens if the van won't be fixed for a few days? What do you guys do then?"

"Between the two bands we're touring with, we can get all of our equipment and us there if need be. The problem is finding time to come back and pick up the van," he said.

Micah's Ember

Ember nodded. She could just imagine how difficult all this must be for them. Their schedule was so hectic, having their only real mode of transportation broken down was the last thing they really needed right now. They were literally playing in a different town, and sometimes even a different state, every night. Having their touring van operational was really a no-brainer.

A thought suddenly occurred to her. "Hey, where the hell are you guys gonna sleep tonight?" she asked, her brow furrowed with worry. She had seen the pics from his social media feeds from previous tours. The band generally camped out in their van, taking turns driving. No van meant no place to sleep, and depending on the costs to fix it, they all could end up totally broke after all this.

Micah shrugged. "I actually hadn't given it much thought. We have our sleeping bags so we can sleep outside. I figure we'll probably just do like we always do and pile on top of each other and sleep best way we can."

Ember tried not to let the worry show in her eyes as she nodded. This all seemed so completely normal for him. She wasn't sure if she should just laugh it off, or feel bad for all of them. It just somehow seemed wrong for them to be traveling around the country in questionable vehicles without much money just hoping they were able to make their way back home again. Yet, she knew this was *exactly* how most bands started out, in raggedy old vehicles with all their hopes and dreams tucked away in the backseat as they rode around the countryside in search of their big break.

He looked at her, as if he had just remembered she was driving around with them this week. "Hey, did you rent another hotel room?"

Micah's Ember

She nodded, a slow smile spreading across her face. "Yes. It's a total roach motel, but when you're buying hotel rooms for an entire week, you kinda have to buy cheap."

He laughed. "You don't have to tell me that. Why do you think we sleep in the van during tours?"

She giggled as she smiled at him. "So you want to bunk with me tonight?"

He propped his arm on the table, resting his chin in his hand as he grinned at her. "Do you even have to ask?"

"I'll take that as a 'yes' then."

He slowly nodded his head, his aquamarine eyes staring into hers. "You about ready to go?" he asked quietly, his voice low.

She returned his stare, her own eyes boring into his as her breathing became slightly labored at the thought of getting him alone again for a few hours. "Hell yeah," she whispered before she stood suddenly, nearly knocking her chair over in her haste.

"What's up?" Spence asked as the two of them got up from the table.

"Me and Em are going to head on out for a while. What's the plan for tomorrow?"

Spence eyed the two of them. He wasn't sure why Micah was hooking up with this chick. He understood the physical attraction; Ember looked damn good considering her age. He still couldn't help but feel one of them was using the other, and he just hoped like hell it was Micah using her and not the other way around.

"We're less than four hours away from our next stop. Danny has agreed to stick around until we find out what's going on with the van. He can haul us and our gear to the next gig if needed.

Micah's Ember

Mechanic shop doesn't open until nine, so I guess just meet us there tomorrow morning?"

Micah nodded as he tossed a twenty on the table. "Sure thing. Call me if you need me."

He grabbed his hoodie off the back of his chair before bidding everyone farewell. Ember couldn't help but notice how Tammy's eyes followed the two of them as they left the table, her mouth slightly ajar as if she hadn't wanted to believe Micah when he insinuated he was with Ember.

It made her smile as they exited the nightclub, Ember resisting the urge to turn around and stick her tongue out at the young girl. Instead, she wrapped her arm around Micah's waist, shoving her hand into his back pocket and squeezing his ass cheek. He hissed slightly at the sudden touch, causing her smile to widen. She could hardly wait to get him alone again so she could have her way with him.

Within a few minutes, the two of them were back in Ember's car heading toward her seedy hotel on the outskirts of town, their hands entwined as they discussed the night's show.

Micah's Ember

Chapter 13

Ember stretched her small body across his, her lips teasing his neck as she slowly kissed her way down the length of him. His skin was so soft, a stark contrast to the hard muscle underneath. He groaned slightly as her teeth grazed his inner thigh. She loved how his body reacted to her touch, loved how his back arched as she slowly popped his cockhead into her waiting mouth, treasured the way he moaned her name as she touched him.

"You are driving me insane," he said as he felt himself slide down her esophagus, the head of dick hitting the back of her throat as she worked more and more of him into her mouth. She had set up a slow and steady alternating rhythm between her mouth and hand, the intense pleasure inside of his body building with each sensuous stroke.

She giggled, the deep vibrations of her mouth sending shock waves through his dick, causing him to moan in pleasure. His reaction only made her giggle harder, his entire body jerking as the sensation ripped through him. Saying she had done things to him he had never dreamed of was most certainly an understatement.

Ember allowed his dick to pop out of her mouth as she slid back up his body to kiss him deeply on the lips, her tongue probing the inner recesses of his mouth. He moved suddenly, flipping

Micah's Ember

her over easily as he wiggled down the bed, grasping her inner thighs with his hands and forcing her legs apart.

"What are you doing?" she gasped, the words barely out of her mouth before she felt his tongue flick across her clit. She nearly screamed at the sensation, her fist shoved between her teeth as his tongue moved in lazy circles around the engorged nubbin, her hips moving in time as the pleasure mounted quickly inside of her, threatening to spill over and consume her at any moment.

"*Fuck*, Micah, you keep doing that and you'll make me come in two seconds flat."

He chuckled as he moved his tongue down to lap at the tangy love juice dripping from her center. "I was right, you do taste delicious," he murmured as he moved his tongue deeper into her body, her hips bucking beneath him.

He replaced his tongue with his finger, the digit delving deep inside as his tongue set back to drawing lazy circles around her clit. He could feel her inner muscles begin to clench as her body shuddered beneath him. He knew it wouldn't be long before she was screaming his name as she rode out her release.

"Micah, *please*," she gasped, feeling the pleasure begin to ripple through her body. He didn't answer, only renewed his efforts with his tongue, loving how her body immediately responded to his touch.

She gasped again before she groaned, her back arched as she wrapped her legs around him, his head held captive as her inner muscles clamped down on his finger. He was rewarded with a gush of warm, sweet nectar as she came in his mouth, his tongue eagerly lapping up her tangy juices.

She groaned when he moved, her body still on fire and demanding more. She shoved him back on

Micah's Ember

the bed as she straddled him, her drenched pussy slowly rubbing along the length of him. She giggled as he grabbed her hips and tried to shove himself into her, but she managed to wiggle out of his grasp.

"So you want to play that game?" he asked with a smirk, one eyebrow raised.

She laughed again as he flipped her over easily, picking her up and pulling her back against him, one hand wrapped loosely around her throat, his other gripping her hip tightly as he kissed the back of her neck.

She groaned again, the heat inside of her nearly scorching in its intensity. She had never wanted someone so badly, didn't think it was possible to want to be taken and owned by another human so completely.

"*Please,*" she begged as an all too familiar sensation ripped through her body.

She knew he was smiling, could almost hear it in his voice as he asked her, "Please what? What do you want, Ember?"

When she didn't immediately answer he slid his hand around her hip, his middle finger quickly finding her clit, causing her to groan again. "Tell me what you want," he said again, his voice more demanding.

"*You,*" she whispered. "I want you, I want you to fuck me, I want to be yours," she said breathlessly as he continued to massage her throbbing clit.

His dick twitched at her words as an odd sense of perverse satisfaction coursed through him. He loved the idea of her being so demanding, being dominated an odd turn on. But feeling her body tremble beneath his, feeling that rush of power from knowing she wanted him, wanted to be *his*, it was a new sensation which sent a rush of

Micah's Ember

heat so intense through his body he thought he would burst.

"Please, Micah, I want to feel you inside me," she moaned, her body on fire as she pressed herself against him, her actions causing her ass to rub against this throbbing cock.

Unable to hold back any longer, he plunged himself into her tight depths, the feel of her body surrounding him nearly taking his breath away.

He buried himself inside of her, quickly setting up a fast and hard tempo as he pounded into her, both of them riding a wave of sheer lust and desire for the other. She met his thrusts eagerly, loving the way he felt inside of her, the minor jolts of pain each time he bottomed out inside of her adding to the intense pleasure quickly building inside.

Within seconds she discovered herself on the edge of oblivion once again, staring off into the black abyss and welcoming it with open arms. She moaned deep inside her throat as he rode her hard and fast, begging him to fuck her deeper as the tingling warmth which started at her inner thighs raged upward, settling into her middle as she screamed out her release, his name a low groan on her lips.

He met each of her movements eagerly, feeling her body tightening around his cock a split second before he, too, tumbled over the edge, his seed spilling forth to drench her insides. His hand held tightly to her hip, his fingers digging into her tender flesh hard enough to leave small bruises, another sensation which kept her moaning in pleasure for several minutes as the two of them finally fell to the bed, exhausted and content, at least for the time being.

"I don't think I could ever get tired of fucking you," he whispered as he wrapped his arms tightly

Micah's Ember

around her waist, his cock still buried deep inside her.

She smiled as she popped on of his fingers into her mouth, her tongue working slow circles around the digit. "I wanted to fuck you as soon as I saw you on Snapagram. I've thought of nothing else, my dreams filled with images of screwing you every way imaginable," she said, her voice low. "Watching you through Skipper just made it worse, wanting to feel your body against mine. Now I just wish we could spend all our time in bed, just fucking until we are both so tired we can't move."

He chuckled. "You're just a cougar aren't you, a spider ready to catch a tasty little fly?"

She smiled, but it was tinged with a bit of sadness. "I don't think of you as being younger than me, to be honest. I understand that's what people see, what they will think of me. They'll see me as someone who is just collecting boy toys to use and toss to the side. But I don't think of you that way."

"You don't think of me as your boy toy?" he asked, feeling his heart flutter inside his chest. As much as he liked the idea of being her own private play thing, his heart yearned for more than just a physical relationship, even though his brain kept reminding him it was an impossible desire. "Then what do you think of me as?" he asked quietly.

She shrugged. "You're Micah. You're someone I enjoy talking to, spending time with. I don't think of the age difference when I think of you, I just think of you as someone I really like, someone I want in my life."

He pulled her closer, kissing the side of her neck. His heart swelled, filled with joy, but he did not answer. He had no idea where this was going, did not know if they had any real future together. She was right about how the world would see

Micah's Ember

them. Even his own band mates thought she was just using him. What would everyone think if they tried to make this relationship work beyond a few quick fucks and some cybersex?

He sighed, his brain shutting down as he finally drifted off to sleep, leaving Ember to stare off into the dim light of the room as her brain circled around the same impossible question.

"When did I start falling in love with you?" she whispered as she lay in his arms, him sleeping contently beside her.

Micah's Ember

Chapter 14

"So what's the deal with you and Micah exactly?" Zachery asked Ember as they stood in the parking lot of the mechanic shop, slowly drinking a much needed latte.

She had dropped Micah off at the shop at nine that morning and went to grab coffee for everyone at a local diner. Now she stood outside the double bay garage doors, waiting with Zachery and Nik and the rest of *Five Days Gone* as Spence and Micah discussed the repairs with the shop owner.

She and Micah both had a lot of reservations about her spending any time with the band apart from their shows. Ember secretly hoped she could win them all over, if they would just give her a chance and stop treating her like a cradle-robbing whore. Despite her best intentions, Micah was pretty sure there was nothing she could say or do which would change Spence's mind about her. Even if Spence did actually like her, he was so sure she was using Micah he just wouldn't let it go. Unfortunately, they all needed her in the off chance their van couldn't be repaired in time to get them to their next show. She thoroughly believed this was the only reason why Spence hadn't already asked her to leave.

Ember took a sip of her coffee, hoping to stall Zachery and his prying questions. She couldn't

Micah's Ember

imagine he really cared one way or the other, especially since she had seen him with at least five different girls in the past two days. She had noticed, with quite some amusement, he had disappeared for more than a half-hour at a time with each of them, cementing her notion he was off in the back somewhere giving them a proper fucking. In all honesty, she had the suspicion all these questions regarding her and Micah's relationship were more for Spence's inquiring mind and less about Zachery actually giving a flying fuck who Micah was screwing.

Micah had told her about the fight with Spence, but he had left out a lot of it. He didn't want her to know just how much Spence distrusted her. It was bad enough he had to put up with all that nonsense from Spence; he hardly felt it was fair to exposure her to any more of Spence's unjustified distrust than was absolutely necessary.

Ultimately he just told her Spence thought she was using him and had concerns. Ember was beginning to think his distrust for her was not rooted in any real evidence, just his general dislike of a much older woman sleeping with a much younger man.

"What do you mean?" she asked after a long pause, wincing at the bitter aftertaste of her coffee. As usual, the waitress hadn't put nearly enough sugar in it for her tastes.

Zachery shoved his hand through his thick curls. He was adorable in that man-boy kind of way, making her want to squeeze him despite his entirely too personal questions making her very uncomfortable. "You know, are you like friends, fuckbuddies, just a rabid groupie, what?"

She stared at him, trying not to laugh as Nik jabbed him in the upper arm while he hissed, "*Dude*, what the fuck?"

Micah's Ember

She took another sip of her coffee before she answered. "Zachery, do you honestly care what Micah and I are doing when we are alone together, or is this a case of *Spence* wanting to know what Micah and I are doing when we are alone together?"

She eyed him as he fidgeted, shifting his weight from one foot to the other. He finally mumbled something under his breath before he turned around and moved toward the open shop doors, looking down at his feet as he walked.

"Sorry about that," Nik said, looking about as uncomfortable and embarrassed about this whole thing as she was.

She shrugged. "Nik, can you answer me something honestly? Would you really care if Micah and I were in a relationship?"

Nik's face turned a bright red as he ducked his head. "Um, um, um." He kept repeating that one sound, over and over again, for what felt like five minutes straight.

She tried not to roll her eyes. What the fuck was with these guys, anyway. They all acted like she was screwing someone underage or something.

Finally Ember interrupted him. "I don't get why everyone is so interested in what Micah and I are doing together. I get the feeling you and Zachery don't give a rat's ass, but Spence just can't seem to let it go. So what the fuck is the deal? Why is everyone so damn concerned about our relationship? Yes, I get that I'm a bit older than him, but for fuck's sake, the man is grown. Don't you think he can make his own decisions?"

Nik looked at her, his face still a bit red. "Honestly, I don't care, and Zachery doesn't care either. As for Spence, I don't really know why he would care. Maybe he's just being overly protective

Micah's Ember

of Micah. It's not you specifically. I just think he's concerned about what could happen to the band."

She looked at him like he was nuts. "What could happen to the band? That doesn't make any sense. What the hell does Spence think I'm going to do, turn him into a house-husband or something? Besides, last time I checked, Spence had a girlfriend. Exactly how is Micah dating someone any different than Spence dating someone?"

Nik shrugged again, obviously at a loss for words.

She sighed, pouring out the last bit of her lukewarm coffee. "Look, you guys have nothing to worry about. The last thing I want is for whatever happens between me and Micah to come between the band or your plans. You guys are awesome, and I really think you have a great shot at making it big. The last thing I want is to cheat Micah out of experiencing that."

She smiled at him, hoping what she was saying was making sense. She really didn't see why any of them were so freaked out by her and Micah. Maybe she was just being stupid, turning a blind eye to what everyone was really thinking.

If she had seen another woman dating a much younger man then she would have immediately thought the woman was being a total hoe-bag with some ulterior motive, even if that ulterior motive was nothing but having a boy toy for a while. And if she had seen an older woman hooking up with a band member, she would immediately have thought the worst as well.

After spending these past few days with Micah coupled with the last five-and-a-half months spent video chatting, she seriously doubted she was able to look at their relationship with any type of unbiased opinion. While her mind knew what

Micah's Ember

everyone else saw and thought, her heart couldn't help but feel they were all blowing things way out of proportion.

"Why do you two look so serious?"

Ember glanced up as Micah approached them, his lips turned up in a lop-sided grin. She returned his smile, immediately feeling at ease as he moved closer to her.

"It's nothing," she said, feeling oddly jubilant as he put his arm around her waist, pulling her closer. "What's the mechanic saying about the van?"

Micah grimaced. "Yeah, it's not good. The transmission is totally shot. It's going to cost more to get it fixed than the van is actually worth. The guy agreed to buy it for scrap, which will give us enough money to rent another van and trailer so we can finish the tour."

"Damn, Micah, that sucks," she said as she wrapped her arms around him waist, feeling a bit perplexed. She knew it was imperative for them to finish this tour. The last thing she wanted was for him to have to cut this week, and thus her visits with him, short. "Is there anything you guys need me to do?"

"No, we're fine," Spence said shortly as he walked up to them, eyeballing her and Micah as they stood with their arms around each other. "We need to go."

Micah, Nik, and Zachery all looked at him. "Where are we going?" Zach asked.

"The Rent-All shop. We need to get a rental and our shit packed so we can hit the road," Spence said.

"Okay, the rest of the guys going to meet us there?" Zachery asked.

"Yeah, now everyone get in the van and let's go. We've got to get on the road."

Micah's Ember

Zachery and Nik followed Spence as he went back to the van where the members of *Five Days Gone* were parked and waiting on the rest of them to get something worked out with their own van. Micah hung back, his arm still wrapped around Ember's waist.

"I'm going to ride with Ember," he said. "You don't mind following us, do you?"

She smiled. "Of course not."

Spence turned back, practically glaring at the two of them. "We need to stick together."

Micah frowned. "Dude, we'll meet you there."

"I'd rather you rode with us."

"Spence, *chill*. We're right behind you. Why are you acting so damn weird all of a sudden?"

Spence raked his hand through his short, spiked brown hair, sighing. "Fine. Just be sure to keep up, okay?"

"Sure," Ember mumbled as she turned to follow Micah to her car. The two of them got into the vehicle, quickly pulling in behind the van.

"What the fuck is Spence's problem?" she finally asked, unable to hide her frustration.

"I honestly have no idea. He's been acting weird as fuck ever since he met you."

"Yeah, I get that, but why? What did you tell them about me?"

"Nothing."

She was quiet for a few moments, not entirely sure she was happy or hurt over his answer. She *knew* he hadn't said anything specific about their relationship, but hearing him admit it hurt her more deeply than she had expected it to. It just reminded her yet again of their age difference and the all-around strangeness of their relationship. She couldn't fault Micah for not wanting to say anything, especially when she didn't even know what was happening between them. As much as

Micah's Ember

her brain knew he was doing the right thing, it didn't make it any easier for her heart to accept it.

"I think it's my age," she finally said, giving voice to the elephant in the room which neither of them had wanted to mention.

He sighed. "They don't even know how old you are. And so what if they did? It's none of their business what I'm doing or who I do it with."

"Yeah, I know, but for whatever reason, Spence has it in for me. Maybe he thinks I'm just a cradle-robbing perv or something."

He tried to smile, but he had been getting the same weird vibe from Spence for the past two days as well. The rest of the guys had been asking him about her off and on, but he had just brushed it off. Zachery and Nik were willing to let it go, but Spence just wouldn't drop it.

"Don't worry about it. He just hasn't had a chance to get to know you. He'll come around, just wait and see."

She nodded, but his words didn't make her feel any better. She wasn't sure what Spence had up his sleeve, but she got the distinct impression he would not sit idly by and let the two of them have any type of relationship outside of their cyber chats.

Micah's Ember

Chapter 15

Ember dropped off Micah at the Rent-All, making sure they had everything they needed before leaving. She had offered to help them transfer their gear and band merchandise into the new rent truck, but Spence had shot her down cold. Not wanting to get into an argument with him, she had finally relented.

She tried to ignore the weird stares she was getting from the rest of the members of *Five Days Gone*, but it was hard. The members of both bands looked decidedly uncomfortable as they all glanced between her and Spence. She knew what they were thinking, no doubt wondering what she had done to piss him off so badly.

Not wanting to make things worse or force Micah into an explanation he wasn't ready to make, she had excused herself, trying her best to smile as she told everyone goodbye. She couldn't imagine things would be much better for Micah once she was gone, but she certainly didn't want to make things worse by hanging around when Spence had made it incredibly clear he did not want her there.

Micah walked her back to her car, promising to call her as soon as they reached their next destination. Feeling frustrated, she had accepted his quick kiss with a smile, even though she felt

Micah's Ember

like crying as she climbed into her car and set her GPS. She found herself short of breath, feeling as if a cold, icy hand was slowly squeezing her heart.

She waved a final goodbye to Micah as she pulled out onto the highway, trying not to think about how awkward things between them had gotten since she had decided to follow the band for the week. Their entire relationship had shifted slightly in the past twenty-four hours, and she couldn't help but feel sad and worried. The thought of their relationship ending wasn't something she was equipped to handle right now, so she shoved it out of her mind. Trying hard not to think about anything so gut-wrenching, she turned her radio up, letting all of her concerns wash away on a cloud of alternative rock.

***

"You are driving me insane, you realize that, right?" Micah said, practically growling low in his throat.

She giggled as she ground herself into him, one leg wrapped around his waist. "All you have to do is unzip your pants and you can slide right inside," she whispered, her tongue lightly tracing the outside curve of his ear.

He shuddered, his dick so hard he thought surely there was going to have permanent nerve damage if he didn't get some type of relief. At the rate he was going, he was going to end up with blue balls before their gig even started.

"Sure you don't want a little taste before your set?" she asked, her lips close to his ear.

He groaned. Fuck it all to hell, he really didn't care who might walk past and see them as they huddled in a dark corner behind the stage. He couldn't take her dry-humping his cock like this.

Micah's Ember

Micah moved suddenly, picking her up and pushing her against the wall, somehow managing to free his throbbing dick with one hand while holding her up with the other. Within seconds he had slipped inside her, both of them groaning as he did so.

She braced herself against the wall, her legs wrapped around his waist as she bounced on his cock, each downward motion causing him to slip deeper and deeper inside her body. He pounded into her, both of them so filled with their desire for each other, neither noticed Spence as he came up behind them, nearly yelping in surprise when he saw his drummer ramming into her in a back corner.

Spence had tried to convince himself there was nothing going on between Micah and this woman, that it was purely infatuation on Micah's part. A kink, an itch to be scratched, maybe a latent desire from wanting to fuck his high school math teacher. As soon as he saw them together, however, he knew his gut had been right all along. There was something more than just a quick fuck going on between them, and judging by the looks on their faces and how they acted around each other, it had been going on for quite some time.

Not really sure what to think or how to handle the situation, Spence slowly and quietly backed away, disappearing down the hall. As upset as he was, he didn't want anyone else to know about what he had just witnessed. He kept hoping once Ember was gone, she would soon be forgotten as their tour continued and Micah was once again surrounded by all the hot, young groupies eager to get into his pants for just one night.

"Harder, Micah, *please*," she groaned, shoving herself down onto his cock and grinding her pubic bone into his.

Micah's Ember

"Damn, doesn't that hurt?" he gasped, not quite sure why she wasn't screaming in pain. The bad thing about being a bit above average in dick size was women tended to only like having their cervix pounded as a kink, not as a steady diet. Ember, however, seemed to love it, and it was just one more thing about her which was slowly causing his insatiable lust for her to deepen.

"*Yes*," she hissed, groaning low in her throat as her orgasm mounted quickly. "But I like it."

Her words caused him to moan as her lips sought his, the two of them kissing fiercely as they climaxed together, his balls emptying inside of her.

"Fuck, I've got to go find the rest of the guys before they coming looking for me," he said as he tried to calm his pounding heart. Despite his words, he made no move to let her go, his arms still holding her against the wall.

"Mmm, dammit, I know. I just can't get enough of you," she said as she kissed him again. She lifted herself off of his dick, feeling his cum already coating the inside of her thighs. She was loath to put her panties back on, but she also didn't want to have to explain why she had semen running down her leg.

"That makes two of us," he said with a chuckle as he stuffed his softening cock back into his jeans. "I'll see you after our set, okay?"

She nodded. "See you then."

He leaned in to kiss her once more and then was gone, leaving her to get cleaned up in the small toilet before joining the packed crowd out on the venue floor.

***

Micah's Ember

"I can't believe you are screwing that woman. Damn, Micah, she's old enough to be your mom for fuck's sake."

Spence stared at Micah in disbelief, wishing his band mate would say something, *anything* other than what was coming out of his mouth.

"First, it's none of your damn business who I'm screwing, and second, so what if I am? You've got a girlfriend back home, and I left mine to drive half-way across the country to join the band. I like Ember, she likes me. So exactly what the fuck is your problem, and how the hell does any of this have anything to do with you? Last time I checked, this was *my* life. Who I choose to see and keep in my life is my business, not yours."

Spence just stared at his drummer as if he had gone crazy. "Are you serious, man? You mean besides the age difference? We are just now getting our foot in the door. What the hell is it going to look like if you are dating a woman damn near twice your age? And why the fuck is she dating you in the first place? I'm all for groupies, dude, but not when they are threatening your career."

"How the fuck is Ember threatening my career?"

"Micah, think about it. You're young, the band is just starting out. She's got her sights set on landing some hot stud and then ride his coattails to stardom, becoming a damn trophy girlfriend or whatever the fuck you want to call her. She's getting older, her biological clock is probably sounding alarm bells or some shit, and what better baby daddy could she hope for than a rock star? She's just using you, dumbass. Why can't you see that?"

"Did you just call Ember a gold-digging whore?" Micah asked through clenched teeth, his eyes narrowed. His heart was racing, and not in a

Micah's Ember

good way. He had never been this angry before. And he couldn't believe Spence could accuse someone he didn't even know of something so damn sleazy.

"Yes, Micah, if you want to get right down to it, I'm calling her a gold-digger. Why else would someone that age want to hang out with a bunch of bands? I mean, I'm all for groupies just as much as the next guy, but at least find some your own age. Does that woman even have a damn job?" Spence's eyes grew wide as a new thought occurred to him. "Oh my fucking God, please tell me you have not been sending money to that skanky bitch."

Micah took a step back, acting as if Spence had physically punched him. He closed his eyes, taking a deep breath and forcing himself to calm down before he punched Spence in the mouth.

"Yes, she has a job you son-of-a-bitch." He glared at Spence, the hurt and anger evident on his face and in his voice. "I can't believe you are accusing her of something like that. You don't even *know* her. And just for the record, *I* came on to *her*, not the other way around. I started this whole thing, despite her protests. So if anyone is to blame for what is going on between us, it's me, because *I* wanted *her*."

Spence shoved his hand through his hair, not really sure which was more disturbing, the fact Ember had let this continue, or the fact Micah had instigated the entire affair. "Exactly what is this thing you are doing anyway? Are you guys like actually dating, just having a fling, what the fuck is going on with you lately?"

Micah shook his head, looking away from Spence. His hands were clenched into fists, and it was all he could do to not shove said fist through the nearest wall. It was bad enough he honestly

Micah's Ember

didn't know what was actually going on with him and Ember. He had never really thought about their relationship past the here and now. But having Spence bring it up and try to force him into some type of decision, to make him put a label on something he didn't really understand himself was pushing all his buttons. Having Ember here in the flesh was only fueling his feelings for her, and it was something he wasn't ready to face just yet.

"Look, I'm only going to tell you this one time, Spence. I consider you to be my brother, but what goes on in my personal life is *my* business, and mine alone. Who I'm sleeping with or who I'm dating is none of your business, *period*. Got it? You have no say-so in the matter. I didn't ask for your opinion, and I don't *want* your opinion. So just drop it before we both say something we'll regret later."

Feeling angry beyond measure, Micah turned and left the backstage area, intent upon putting as much space between himself and Spence as possible. He had worked too hard to jeopardize his relationship with his band mates. Rather than continue the fight, he thought it best if he just dropped the matter and spent some time away from Spence, even if it meant letting him think the worst of Ember.

Between Spence's unwanted judgement and his own troubling feelings toward Ember leaving far too many questions unanswered, his anger was quickly burning out of control. His inability to face his true feelings for Ember was causing him just as much concern as anything Spence had said this past week.

***

Micah's Ember

"Where have you been? I've looked all over this place for you. Some of the fans are getting a bit antsy," Ember said as she finally caught up with Micah after their show.

She had been trying to get backstage since the end of their set, but the venue they were at had actual security guards who refused to let anyone backstage. She had spent nearly fifteen minutes arguing with the guy, knowing full damn well he had seen her come in with the band and saw her exit the backstage area before the concert. Despite all this, he still refused to let her go backstage. His excuse was, "I've been told by the band no one is to come backstage. They will all be coming out after their various sets to visit with the fans. Please take a seat and stop trying to cause a riot."

Ember had finally given up, but not before she had told the security guard, rather rudely, "I'm not a damn fan, you asswipe, I'm Micah's girlfriend."

As soon as the words had left her mouth, she regretted them. Not because she didn't want to actually *be* his girlfriend, but because she still had no idea how Micah was classifying their relationship to himself or to his band mates. The last thing she wanted was to come off as some psycho cougar groupie with a drummer fetish.

She stopped as she got closer to Micah, immediately noticing how annoyed he looked. She was so used to him being all smiles, laughing and joking about everything that seeing him frowning and in an obviously bad mood immediately sent alarm bells off inside her head. Something was wrong, and she was pretty damn sure Spence was at the center of whatever it was.

"What's wrong?" she asked, reaching out to gently put her hand on his arm.

She could feel him flinch, as if he were resisting the urge to jerk away from her. She heard

Micah's Ember

him sigh slightly as he rubbed the back of his head. "Nothing, just tired. It's been a long week."

She tried not to frown as she nodded. It was just Tuesday, but he had also been on tour for nearly three months now. She imagined he was probably getting worn out, and the fact she had been screwing him senseless every chance she got instead of letting him sleep probably wasn't helping any.

"What's the plan for tonight?" she asked with a smile, opting not to bring up his odd behavior. She didn't want to sound pushy or upset him any more than what he already was. Her visit was supposed to have made him happy, not drive a wedge between him and the band, although she had a growing fear her presence was doing just that despite her best efforts to not get in the way.

He shrugged. "We've got close to a ten hour drive ahead of us. We're leaving around midnight, take turns driving until we get to the next venue."

"Do you want to stay with me tonight? I had planned to hit the road around seven, drive straight through."

He stared at her, debating on his answer. He wanted to spend the night with her more than anything right now. The thought of spending the next ten hours stuck inside the Rent-All van with Spence grilling him about his relationship with her had his stomach tied in knots and his heart cutting cartwheels inside his chest, and not in a good way.

He had much rather spend that time with her, but he also knew if he did then it would just make things worse between him and Spence. The last thing he needed was for anything to come between him and his band mates. It sucked, having to choose between the woman he wanted to spend time with and not causing a rift between the band.

Micah's Ember

"I would love you, Em, but I can't. We'd end up fucking all night, not get any sleep, probably be late for the show because we were forced to pull over and take a nap." He tried to smile to soften his words, but he felt like shit, emotionally and physically.

Finally being able to hold Ember in his arms had been more wonderful than he ever imagined. He had dreamed about the day when he could meet her in person, to feel her body pressed against his. Finding her out in the audience Sunday night had been one of the happiest moments of his life. Having her here with him was literally a dream come true for him. Unfortunately, Spence was taking what should have been one of the happiest times of his life and corrupting it with his questions, his suspicions, and his unfounded accusations. The past few days had left him emotionally drained and physically ill.

She nodded, her head bent slightly so he couldn't see the pain in her eyes. "You're probably right. Neither of us has gotten much sleep the past two nights."

She looked up, forcing a bright smile onto her face. "It's fine. I'll go back to the hotel, get some sleep, and meet up with you tomorrow night. That sound good?"

He reached down, pulling her into his arms and kissing her softly. She melted into his embrace, her body immediately making demands despite her heart feeling like it was being ripped in two.

"Dammit," she whispered when he finally released his hold on her mouth.

"What's wrong?" he asked in concern.

"You should know by now that you touching me sets my body on fire," she whispered, her arms still wrapped around his neck.

Micah's Ember

He grinned at her, his anger at Spence slowly seeping away as he held the object of his affection in his arms. "Really?" he asked, leaning down to gently brush his lips across hers.

She groaned, relieved to see him smiling. "No fair, you're going to be leaving soon and you still have fans to meet."

"So you don't mind me meeting fans?" he asked, using the opportunity to pick her brain on exactly how she felt about having to share him with the people who came out to support them as musicians.

"No, it's your job. You play music, you make fans, they spread the word, and if you are really lucky, you get a huge following and record deals and before you know it, you're swimming in groupies. Kinda goes with the scene."

"You think I'll get groupies?" he asked teasingly.

"If you're lucky. Probably a bunch of cougars too," she said with a grin.

He laughed. "Won't you be jealous of the groupies and the cougars?"

She shrugged. "I can share when I have to," she said, grinning at him.

"Oh, you're into sharing are you?"

"Sure, I'll share your smile, a hug, lots of pictures. Hell, I might even be willing to share a kiss or two, but this," she said as she stealthily grabbed hold of his cock through his pants, "this is *mine*, remember?"

He gasped when he felt her hand squeezing his dick through his pants, a low moan escaping his lips. "Yes, ma'am," he whispered, leaning down to kiss her hard as a shudder of pleasure traveled through his body.

He could just imagine how things would be for them if they became exclusive. She'd have a fetish

Micah's Ember

collar around his neck and a cock ring around his balls, a gentle reminder that no matter how many groupies he took photos with or how many women tried to grab hold of his ass after a show, his cock, his *heart*, would always belong to her.

The scenes dancing around inside his head sent a shockwave of pleasure through his body. Just the thought of being hers for the rest of his life made his heart beat just a little bit faster.

"I've got to go," he finally said, his forehead pressed against hers as he stared into her eyes.

"I know. Go meet some fans, sign some autographs. I'll see if I can find a table and have a drink or two. If you get a chance, drop by. And be sure to let me know when you guys are leaving. I demand a goodbye kiss before you go," she said with a smile, letting him know she was only half-way joking about the kiss.

He nodded, reluctantly letting her go before disappearing into the crowd. She sighed, watching as he moved among the patrons, laughing as he was immediately surrounded by supporters of the band.

Feeling alone, she made her way to the bar, ordering a mixed drink and asking for another round to be sent to her table. She settled down in her seat, watching as all the young women moved around the different band members, her feeling incredibly old and out of place.

How could I have ever thought I would fit into his life? she wondered to herself, her heart heavy with doubt and unanswered questions.

***

It was nearly two in the morning, and Ember had done nothing over the past ninety minutes but toss about in her bed. She had spoken to Micah for

Micah's Ember

the first fifteen minutes after they had all left the venue, but he was tired and neither of them really wanted to say anything which would cause Spence to start on another round of Twenty Questions.

She flopped over onto her back, staring up at the ceiling with unseeing eyes. She had never felt so alone, the feeling so tangible it was literally making her sick to her stomach. She had never missed anyone this badly, her heart feeling as if it were being ripped out of her chest.

She had spent the last two hours fighting back tears, first when she had been forced to say goodbye to Micah outside the club, then again when they had ended their conversation. Now as she lay in the bed, she could feel the backs of her eyes stinging. She blinked a few times, but it was no use. Her heart was breaking, and she gave in to the rush of emotions, curling up on her side as the tears cascaded down her cheeks.

How was it possible to miss someone this much? If she felt this miserable after only three days spent around him, how bad was it going to be when she was forced to go back to work, to go back to her real life, and not be able to see him in the flesh on a daily basis? And what would she do when this relationship of theirs finally came to an end, when the novelty of having an online affair with an older woman wore off and he cut all ties with her?

The thought of never seeing him again, of never hearing his voice again brought on a fresh bought of tears. What was happening to her? When had she fallen so deeply in love with someone who could drop her just as easily as he had picked her up?

The unfairness of it all ripped through her as her own inner voice rang inside her head – *what a fool you are.*

Micah's Ember

Chapter 16

It was close to six the next evening when Ember finally made it to her hotel room. It had taken her a bit longer than anticipated to drive to the next venue. She was so tired from a restless night she could barely concentrate, making an already long journey a nearly endless endeavor.

At five that morning, after being unable to fall asleep, she had given up on trying to get any rest and checked out of her hotel, spending the next six hours on the road. She had spoken with Micah for a few minutes at lunch, but that had been the last time she had heard from him. She had pulled into a rest stop around one that afternoon, getting a few hours of sleep in before she finished up the last leg of her drive.

Now she felt like warmed over death, and the fact she hadn't heard anything out of Micah since earlier in the day was adding to her foul mood. All she wanted to do was get checked into her hotel room and get a few more hours of sleep until the show.

As she pulled into the parking lot of her hotel, she was shocked to see *Tempered Souls'* Rent-All van sitting in the parking lot. She parked her car, feeling the dread wash over her like a cold bucket of water, the sensation leaving her sick at her stomach and her legs feeling like limp noodles.

Micah's Ember

Micah was standing outside her car before she had a chance to open the door. She tried hard to muster a smile as she got out, but there was no way to mask the worry etched into her expression. She heaved a sigh of relief when he pulled her into his arms and kissed her long and hard.

"Surprised to see me?" he asked huskily as he reluctantly let go of her.

She giggled. "Yeah, and worried to be honest. What's going on?"

"Ugh, more bad news. Our booking agent booked the wrong venue, so it looks like we have the night off."

She looked at him with a furrowed brow. "What do you mean, they booked the wrong venue?"

He grimaced. "Apparently there are two venues with the same name. When our agent was booking our shows, he didn't realize it so he booked a venue with the same name in a different state. Not quite sure how the hell he managed it, but there ya go."

She snorted, trying hard not to laugh. It sounded like something she would do. "Well that sucks," she said.

"Yeah, but in his defense he did try to get us booked at the right venue. Unfortunately, they didn't have an opening."

"Damn, first the van and now this shit. I'm beginning to think I'm jinxing you guys or something."

He laughed before pulling her closer. "Naw, this kind of shit happens all the time. The van breaks down at least twice each time we tour. I guess it was about time we had to put it out to pasture."

Micah's Ember

She smiled as she pressed herself against him. "Well, at least you have the night off, so that's some good news right?"

He nodded. "Yes, a night off sounds wonderful. Three months and the only time we've had off was because we were driving to the next gig. It just sucks because we don't get paid if we aren't playing."

"Mmm. You know, you are something else, Micah Vaughn."

"I am?" he asked, giving her a lop-sided grin. "Why do you say that?"

"Because you keep doing this even though you are constantly being thrown curve balls. You keep working, you stay positive, and you keep pushing for your dreams, no matter what life throws at you. That is very rare in this day and age. Most everyone just assumes life owes them everything."

He shrugged. "That's the only way you are going to amount to anything in this world, you know, work your ass off and then get up and do it all again the next day. You have to just keep pushing and working, never give up, never stop believing in your dreams."

She leaned in and kissed him again, feeling her heart swell. She really was proud of him. And as much as she felt her heart twitch with a tiny twinge of jealousy each time she saw a new girl drape herself across him like a cheap coat, she still felt proud knowing he was living his dream. She couldn't imagine him doing anything else, and she really did hope he would make it in this all-too often cold and heartless industry.

"So, you finally have a night off. What's the plan?" she asked after a few seconds.

"Would you be incredibly pissed if I just wanted to hole up in a hotel room and not do a thing but eat junk food and watch cheese flicks?"

Micah's Ember

She giggled. "Actually, that sounds wonderful to me." She paused before asking, "What about the rest of the band? Where are they, by the way? And do you guys need a place to crash for the night?"

"Oh, no, Spence rented us a room for the night." He grinned at her. "It's going to be pretty crowded in there with the other guys. Don't suppose you mind me crashing with you instead?"

A slow, seductive smile spread across Ember's face. "Do you even have to ask?"

***

Micah and Ember sat side-by-side in the bed, surrounded by various chip bags, candy, and cupcake wrappers. They had spent the last eight hours alternating between taking half hour naps and screwing each other senseless until finally, their desires were sated and their need for rest and food took over their need for each other.

"So what did you do in high school?" she asked as she shoved another bite of beef jerky into her mouth.

"What do you mean?" he asked, reaching across her to grab another bag of chips.

"What were you like? Did you play football, were you one of the preppy kids? Or were you one of the grunge kids who played in a garage band and stole your sister's eyeliner?"

Micah laughed at the images her questions were invoking inside of his mind. "I didn't have a sister to steal eyeliner from and I did not play football. My dad always tried to get me to do it, but I was too scared I would break my arm and not be able to play drums. We butted heads about it through junior high, but once I managed to get him to actually see my band play, he stopped

Micah's Ember

trying to get me to join the football team. Sort of a mutual truce, so to speak."

"A truce? How's that?"

"Well, I agreed not to grow my hair out or put on a skirt, and he agreed to stop harassing me about joining a sports team."

She giggled, trying to imagine him with long hair and a skirt. There was just no way; he didn't have the body type to carry off that kind of look.

"So you always knew you wanted to be a musician?"

"Oh hell yeah," he said as he took another swallow of cola. "I scored my first drum kit from an estate sale when I was thirteen. Drove my parents crazy those first few years. But that's how I ended up with my room moved into a soundproofed basement, so you know, silver lining."

"They made you move into the basement?"

"Yeah, but it was great. It was half the size of the house so I had my bedroom on one end and all my musical equipment on the other. Me and my band could practice all we wanted without disturbing my parents or the neighbors."

"What was the name?" she asked, really enjoying talking to him about something other than how much she wanted to fuck him.

"Name of what?"

"The band," she said with a laugh. "What was the name of the band?"

"Carpathian Sanity," he said as he winced.

She raised an eyebrow. "Seriously?

He nodded as he laughed. "Yeah, and we went through a *lot* of names before we settled on that one."

"Really? Well now you gotta tell me what those names were. If Carpathian Sanity won the vote, I want to know what was tossed to the side."

Micah's Ember

He rolled his eyes. "Ugh, some of them were just horrible."

"That's what I'm counting on," she said with a laugh.

"Fine. Let's see," he said as he cocked his head to the side, trying to remember some of the names they had tossed around all those years ago. "Vital Battle, Fox Alive, Steel Insanity, Screams of Winter, Nuclear Coffin, Unholy Unicorn ..."

She groaned. "Yeah, you're right, they're all pretty horrible. Although I kinda like Nuclear Coffin."

He grinned at her. "That was one of my ideas."

They sat in silence for a few minutes, happily munching on the various snacks scattered around them. "What about you?" he asked.

"What about me?"

"What were you like in high school? Were you always this fun-loving?"

Ember shook her head as she swallowed a bite of cupcake. "God, no. I was terribly unpopular, a total nerd. I was tied for salutatorian of my class, spent my days reading and studying. A total introvert."

He looked her over, trying to wrap his head around the scenario she was painting of herself. "Sorry, I just don't believe it. Why would you waste your teenage years locked in your room studying?"

"I was on a mission," she said as she began to gather up the candy wrappers.

"A mission? For what?"

She shrugged. "To get a good job, to be self-sufficient. We were pretty poor, which made me a target for bullies as it was. All I could think about was if I got a good education I'd be able to get a good paying job. For years my only goal in life was to walk back into my high school reunion driving a beamer and flipping them off."

Micah's Ember

He looked at her as if he were seeing her for the first time. "Damn. Okay, so did you?"

She snorted. "You've seen my car. I barely make twenty-five grand a year."

"So what happened?" he asked, genuinely curious.

"I got tired of school. Guess you could say I got burnt out. Then I met someone, got engaged, quit school."

"Wait, hold up, you were engaged?" he asked, his mouth popping open.

Ember laughed. "Yeah, why are you so surprised?"

"I don't know, I mean, I'm not surprised you were engaged. I always assumed you were divorced or something. Never crossed my mind that you hadn't ever been married."

"Ah, no, never made it that far."

"So you're not divorced?"

She shook her head. "No, we were engaged for a few years, but he was one of those guys who was content with whatever life handed him, you know? Like he had no drive, no passion, didn't want anything more out of life. He came from a poor family and his only goal was to earn enough to pay taxes."

She took a sip of cola before continuing. "I was okay with that for a while. After working my ass off for so many years and not really having anything to show for it but stress ulcers, it was nice to just roll with whatever life threw at us. But, after working dozens of dead-end jobs and not be able to pay our bills most of the time, I decided something had to change. He wasn't interested in trying for a better life, and I was sick of never being able to make ends meet. So we broke up, I went back to college, finished my degree, and have been trying to climb the corporate ladder ever since. Which, for

Micah's Ember

the record, doesn't technically exist for anyone who doesn't already come in toward the top of the company."

"Damn, sorry things didn't work out," he said, although he was silently wondering if she thought he was the same way.

"Don't be. I learned a lot about myself after we broke up, and about what I really wanted and needed out of life."

"Like what?" he asked, thoroughly intrigued by the little strawberry blonde sitting beside him in the bed.

"Like money can't buy happiness. Don't get me wrong, it's nice not to have to worry about paying bills," she said with a laugh. "But money isn't everything. As much as I enjoy buying nice things, it won't buy you the things in life that really count, like family and people you can count on to be there for you."

"I guess me and Jonathan were just at opposite ends of the spectrum," she continued. "I was all drive and ambition, and he had none to speak of. It took me several years to realize you can't spend all your time working and worrying about finances and trying to get ahead in the world."

She paused again as her face took on a far-away look as she peeled back the layers of time. "You never get to really enjoy or experience anything when you are like that. So I stopped focusing so much on my career and started paying more attention to my hobbies, to *life*. I started back with photography and graphic art, got back into music, and just started being the real me for the first time since high school."

He listened to all of this intently, nodding his head. He understood what she meant. "I get it. I've worked my ass off to get where I'm at, but I still

Micah's Ember

remember to enjoy every minute of it. So many bands fail before they make it. Even if we never hit it big, I'm still living my dream, even if that means living out of a van six months out of the year."

They laughed together, sitting quietly as they reflected on their lives up to this point. "Does it bother you?" he asked after a few minutes.

"Does what bother me?"

"Me being in the band. You know, not having a regular job, being hugged and kissed and having women constantly trying to shove their hands down my pants?"

She giggled. "Women try to shove their hands down your pants?"

He ducked his head, blushing in embarrassment. "Yeah, I've had that happen quite a few times."

Ember smiled at him. "No. I mean, yes, I do feel a bit jealous, but I feel more proud, knowing you've worked so hard to get to this point. I get that being in a band means you get touched a lot so no, I'm not like going to flip out because you are hanging out with your fans. You work hard, and you deserve everything that hard work brings your way."

"Oh, that reminds me," she said suddenly, grabbing a napkin and wiping her hands and mouth. "I brought you something."

"You got me something?" he asked, watching as she ducked into the bathroom.

"Yeah, I brought it with me just in case," she said as she rummaged through her overnight bag.

A few seconds later she emerged from the other room, settling back into the bed beside him. She handed him a long, thin box, smiling shyly as she did so.

Micah's Ember

"You didn't have to get me anything," he said as he took the box from her, carefully opening it to peek inside.

"Well, technically I bought it a few months ago. I know I said I wasn't going to bring it up, but since I'm not sure when we'll get to see each other again." She shrugged, the thought causing the sadness to slowly grip her heart.

Micah opened the box, his eyes growing a little wide as he saw the little leather bracelet nestled inside. He picked it up, immediately recognizing it as the one she had shown him via one of their earlier Skipper conversations.

He held it in his hand, reading over the simple inscription on the silver plate – OWNED BY MISTRESS.

He grinned at her. "I can't believe you still have this, and brought it to me."

She giggled. "Well, I did buy it for you, even if it was a joke at the time. You should have it."

He smiled as he set the bracelet on the night stand next to his phone, pulling her closer so he could kiss her. "Thank you. I must admit I've never had a gift quite like it, or known anyone quite like you."

He pulled her into his arms as they snuggled together beneath the covers. He had sacrificed everything when he moved out to Michigan to join *Tempered Souls*. He had expected for this to be a wondrous albeit a very lonely road. He never dreamed he would meet someone who not only knew what came with dating someone in a rock band, but who was willing to roll with all the punches this life threw at her.

Micah's Ember

Chapter 17

"I can't believe this shit is happening," Spence said as he grasped his head with both hands, his dark brown eyes looking around as if he wasn't sure if he wanted to start screaming or crying.

"It's going to be okay," Micah said.

Spence turned around quickly before Micah barely had the words out of his mouth. "No, it's *not* going to fucking be okay, Micah. All of our shit was in that van. Our equipment, our merchandise, our clothes, *every* fucking *thing*. We are so screwed!"

Ember winced, biting her tongue. Spence had been raving about their Rent-All van being stolen for the past hour. Even after they had filled out the police report and given a thorough account of everything which was inside the van, he was still absolutely beside himself over it. She understood they were all upset, but Spence's tirade was quickly spiraling out of control.

"This is all your fault," Spence said suddenly as he took a step toward Micah. "If it hadn't been for you insisting we stay in the same roach motel as your little fuckbuddy, none of this shit would have happened."

"Now wait just a damn minute," Ember said before she even realized she had opened her mouth to speak. She knew she should stay out of this, but she wasn't about to stand around and let Spence

Micah's Ember

attack Micah just because he was upset. "How the hell is any of this Micah's fault? Exactly where the fuck would you all have ended up last night if you hadn't stopped here? I didn't see you taking the rest of the band to a different hotel. No one forced you to stay here."

Spence spun around to glare at her. "Stay the fuck out of this, you bitch. This doesn't concern you."

"Whoa, hold the fuck up, man. You are not going to speak to her like that," Micah said, getting in between Ember and Spence.

Ember refused to back down, and she stepped from behind Micah to glare up at Spence. "You start blaming Micah for shit that isn't his fault and yeah, you bet your tattooed ass it's my business. Micah didn't force any of you to stay here, and neither did I. You could just as easily have dropped him off and went somewhere else to get a hotel. It's not his fault or mine that some asshole stole your rental van and made off with your shit. Yes, it fucking sucks so damn bad I can't even imagine what all of you are going through right now, but blaming each other won't fix the problem."

Spence looked at her for a second before he nodded his head. "You know, you're right. It's not Micah's fault, it's *your* fault. Micah has been acting weird for months now and it's all because he's been screwing around with you all this time. If you hadn't followed him out here and tried to worm your way into his life, none of us would be stuck here right now. Instead, we'd be half-way to our next gig, laughing and joking about being on the road."

"This isn't Ember's fault, Spence, and you know it. And I don't appreciate you speaking to her like this. She's helped us out more than once this week. She didn't have to stick around to make sure

Micah's Ember

we made it to our next gig, but she did. And your way of thanking her is by accusing her of something she had no control over? What the fuck is your problem, man?"

"You want to know what my problem is?" Spence asked, his eyes narrowed as he glared at Micah. "My problem is that my drummer has lost his damn mind. You are chasing after a dried up piece of pussy that's old enough to be your mom and in the meantime, you are blowing off practice sessions, you are abandoning your band to go screw this wannabe groupie, and for what? Why the hell would you jeopardize the life you have worked so hard for all for the sake of screwing some random woman you met online?"

"That's not fair, Spence," Micah said through clenched teeth. His hands were balled into fists, and it was all he could do not to punch his singer in the mouth.

"I've already told you it was none of your damn business who I see, who I date, or who I sleep with. Half the time your girlfriend is tagging along with us on tour and you don't hear any of us complaining about it. Exactly what the hell do you have against Ember? You've not said one civil thing to her this whole week. You haven't even *tried* to get to know her. The only thing you seem to care about is her age. Why is that? Do you secretly have some type of mommy fetish? Are you jealous she's a better lay than your own girlfriend? Or are you still pissed about your ex-girlfriend leaving you at the altar? Is that it? Are you so hung up over your own experiences with an older woman that you would rather sabotage someone's relationship than see them happy?"

Ember didn't realize what Spence intended to do until she heard the loud *crack* of his fist landing against Micah's cheek. She screamed, feeling her

Micah's Ember

heart jump into her throat as she rushed over to Micah. He held up his hand, stopping her before she could get any closer.

"*This* is how you solve problems? By punching your friends?"

Spence stood his ground, his breath labored as he glared at his drummer. "No. The problem in this band is your little girlfriend over there. So it's time to make a decision, Micah. Her or the band. You either stay in this band, reap the rewards we have all sacrificed for these past two years, or you can go home with her and start working at a local factory, get married, have some kids for all the fuck I care. But you can't have both, Micah, not when you are the only one who wants her around. So choose. The band, or your girlfriend."

"That's not fair, Spence. You have your girlfriend back home, and Ember lives over a thousand miles away from me. How is our relationship hurting this band? She came out to support us on tour for a damn week. She bought tickets and merch when she didn't have to. I don't see how making me choose is going to change a fucking thing with this band."

"Then obviously you are even more blind to what's been going on the past few months than I thought. You aren't sleeping, you're blowing off practice, you only half-ass pay attention to what we've been discussing for the new album, and now you are disappearing after shows to spend time with her. I may have a girlfriend, Micah, but she doesn't control my life-"

"Ember isn't controlling my life," Micah interrupted, his voice low in his anger.

"Yes, she does. You may not realize it, you may not see it as such, but she does. You are rearranging your entire life around her schedule so you can spend time chatting with her. That means

Micah's Ember

we are having to rearrange our entire work schedule for the band around her as well. And we can't keep doing that if we expect to make it as a band, Micah, and you know it."

Micah stood staring at Spence, wishing his words didn't hold some grain of truth to them, but they did. He knew he had been blowing off the rest of them to spend time video chatting with Ember. Trying to carry on a relationship with someone who lived across the country from him was a lot harder than dating someone who lived in the same city. It wasn't like she could be there during practice sessions or when they were discussing their next album or going over their marketing expenses. She was a distraction, even if it was a distraction he desperately wanted in his life, she was still something that was obviously coming between him and all the hard work he had put into this band over the years.

The tightness inside Ember's chest felt like it was going to crush her where she stood. She hadn't wanted to admit it, but Spence was right, about everything. She had known Micah was making excuses to brush off the rest of the band so he could spend time on video chats with her, but she had somehow thought it was all going to be okay.

She knew it was happening, and yet she had excused it away instead of saying something, all because she wanted to spend as much time with him as possible. She had convinced herself this wasn't just some random thing to occupy Micah's time. She had let herself believe this relationship could become something more than just a cyber fling.

What a fool she had been, chasing after someone so much younger than herself. Foolish, naïve, and selfish.

Micah's Ember

Micah turned to look at Ember, and she could already see it in his eyes. The regret, the confusion, but more importantly, he was looking at her the same way Spence had looked at her, like she was someone who had been purposely using him for her own selfish reasons.

She blinked, fighting back the tears which threatened to take over. They were right, and she knew it. She was being so selfish, and it was time she stopped.

"He's right, Micah. You've worked too hard to just piss it all away. I've been selfish, wanting to keep you to myself," she said quietly before she turned to Spence, the unshed tears glittering in her eyes. "I told you I wasn't going to come between Micah and the rest of the band, and I meant it."

Micah took a step toward her, but she backed up, shaking her head. "No, Micah. I've been a fool. Everyone will always see us the same way the rest of the band sees us. They'll all think I'm just another gold-digging whore trying to get my claws into a younger man. They'll think I'm just using you for your fame and your money. I'm not going to let you throw away your dreams on something so hopeless."

She took another step back, her arms crossed over her chest as she swallowed the lump in her throat which was threatening to suffocate her. "I'm sorry, Micah. I should never have let this get so far out of control. I should have known better. You deserve your dreams, and you deserve to share them with someone who can stand by your side and help the band get to where it deserves to be, not have someone who is only dragging you down. You deserve so much more than just some dried up old cougar having a midlife crisis."

She turned, fumbling in her pocket for her keys. "I'm sorry, but I'm not going to let you throw

Micah's Ember

all this away over someone you may not even want in a few months." She pulled her keys out of her pocket, wrapping her arms around her chest again.

"Goodbye, Micah," she whispered softly before she turned, walking quickly to her car. She did not give him a chance to say anything, didn't wait to see if he would come running after her. All she wanted was to get out of the parking lot as fast as possible before the tears began and the crushing loneliness rushed up to embrace her.

Micah's Ember

Chapter 18

Ember sat at her computer staring blankly at her screen. She had driven straight back home, more than eight hours, without stopping. Somehow she had managed to block out everything which had just happened, but as soon as she walked into her house, she broke down, the sobs wracking her small body. She had cried until she had vomited and there were no more tears to shed. She spent the entire weekend repeating the cycle, crying until she finally fell asleep out of sheer exhaustion only to wake up and begin crying all over again.

It had been two months now since she had heard anything from Micah. She kept hoping and praying he would text her, call her, anything, but he had completely cut her out of his life. She wished she could forget about him as easily as he seemed to have forgotten about her. But no matter how hard she tried to shove him out of her mind, her nights were still haunted by aquamarine eyes and an infectious smile, her days filled with a bitter emptiness she wasn't sure she could handle.

For weeks afterward she tried to talk herself into calling him, to apologize, to beg him to at least consider her a friend. She knew, deep in her heart, she couldn't bear having him in her life as anything other than the man she loved, the man she wanted to spend the rest of her life with.

Micah's Ember

Trying to carry on any type of friends-only relationship with him would be just too painful for her.

She half-expected him to call, to text, but as the days continued on in an endless cycle of torment without a single word from him, she slowly realized he couldn't possibly have felt the same way about her as she did about him. It was a sobering thought which left her heartbroken and floundering in a sea of doubt. So she had resisted the urge to call him, praying the heartbreak would eventually subside.

She kept telling herself to just give it time, but as the days filtered into weeks, the weeks into months, the heartache she felt today was just as fresh and painful as it had been the last day she had seen him. Now she sat at her computer, too drained to concentrate on anything. She did nothing but go to work and come home. Her graphic artwork, her photography, none of it held any happiness for her any more. All she felt was a gnawing emptiness inside of herself, stretching out into infinity. Pain, regret, an abyss of loneliness staring back at her was her only companion these days.

She sighed, finally getting up from her computer to wander around the house aimlessly, wondering if her life would ever get back to normal. She didn't understand how she could have gotten so emotionally involved with someone she had literally only spent four days with. At what point had she started falling for him, exactly when had he become such an integral part of her life that trying to exist without him was more painful than anything she could possibly imagine?

***

Micah's Ember

"What's wrong with you, Em?" Nicci asked at lunch a few weeks later. The two of them sat at their usual booth in the small diner, Em picking at the salad in front of her.

"What?" Em asked, looking up at her friend with empty eyes.

"Damn, Ember, what the fuck is going on with you lately? You've been a ghost of yourself for three months now. You've lost so much weight you are beginning to look sick, you have bags under your eyes big enough to pack for a weekend getaway, your skin is so sallow you look like a damn candlestick. I swear I don't think you even *bother* to try to fix your hair anymore. I hate to say it, sweetie, but you look like total shit. What the hell happened while you were on vacation? I thought you were supposed to come back looking tan and rejuvenated, not like you visited a concentration camp."

She shrugged. "It's nothing," she said absently as she went back to picking at her salad, not really seeing it.

"Twenty pounds lost and a sallow complexion is not 'nothing,' Em." Nicci reached across the table to touch Ember's hand, the concern in her friend's eyes evident. "You know you can tell me anything, right? No judgement. Is it that drummer you were chatting with?"

Ember stared at Nicci for a second, the warm wall of denial she had wrapped herself in suddenly crashing down around her in grand style. Her face crumpled, her hands over her face as she cried, trying desperately to compose herself. "Nicci, I'm such a damn fool," she said in between the sobs.

"Em, hon, no you're not. What happened? Did he turn out to be a total twat waffle or something?"

Micah's Ember

The sentiment made Ember cry harder, reminding her of everything she had been through in the past nine months of her life. "No, and yes."

"Alright, hon, spill it, from the beginning."

Ember sniffled, taking a napkin and blotting at the mascara-stained tears running down her cheeks. She took a few seconds to compose herself, and then she told Nicci everything which had happened, from the beginning of their weird cyber relationship all the way through the four days she had spent with him while on tour.

"How could I have been so stupid, Nicci? I'm damn near old enough to be this kid's mother. How could I have ever thought I could mean anything to him other than a fling? I knew better than to get involved with him, but I did it anyway. And the further into it we got, the more I kept rationalizing it to myself that it was just for fun."

Nicci regarded her friend for a few seconds. "You're in love with him, aren't you?" she asked quietly.

Ember's large blue eyes looked her, the tears immediately spilling down her cheeks all over again. "How the fuck did this happen, Nicci? How the hell does a woman pushing forty fall in love with a twenty-two year old she has literally spent four days with?"

Her friend smiled, patting her hand. "Oh, hon, you may have only physically been in his presence for four days, but you spent five plus months chatting with him. Was it always about getting off, or did you guys have actual conversations?"

Ember sniffled, dabbing at her nose. "It started out just being about sex. The whole first month we screwed ourselves senseless. But his schedule was so hectic with them getting ready for tour that a lot of chats were too short for anything else, so it was us just shooting the shit, you know? His life, my

Micah's Ember

life, hobbies, work." She shrugged. "I just miss him, you know? I miss his face, his voice, his laugh. God, I'd just about sell my soul to hear his voice again, to see that sweet smile of his."

"Em, I hate to be a bitch, but exactly what did you expect to happen with this relationship? Age aside, you two live on opposite sides of the country. Even if you were still chatting with him, where was the relationship going anyway? You can't expect him to be content with having a girlfriend he never gets to touch."

She groaned. "I know, Nicci, I know. It's why I keep telling myself to just let it go, move on. There's no way I would ever ask him to give up on his dreams to move down here to this backwater town."

"Have you thought about moving up there with him?"

Ember looked at Nicci like she was crazy. "And do what? He lives with Spence and his girlfriend, and I think Zachery lives there, too. What am I supposed to do to support myself? I've clawed my way out of the pits of hell to get to where I am right now. I can't imagine my job opportunities would be any better up there than they are around here. I don't have nearly the education or the experience, and I damn sure don't have any connections."

"You know you can do your job from anywhere in the world, right? And there's no way Tanner would fire you; he depends on you too much."

"Okay, so let's say for argument's sake that I could move up there and keep my job. That still doesn't change the fact I'm seventeen years older than him. It still doesn't change the fact Spence hates me, or that he thinks I'm just a gold-digger looking for a free ride. It doesn't change the fact that everyone who sees us will automatically think the worst of me because I'm dating someone so

Micah's Ember

much younger than me. And it still doesn't change the fact I obviously feel more for Micah than he feels for me. So all of this is a moot point. I've just got to nut-up and somehow manage to get over him."

"Is that possible, Em? We only get one shot at love in our lives. Do you really want to let this chance slip through your fingers because you are afraid of what people may think about your relationship?"

Ember sat quietly for a few minutes. "It's not just about me, Nicci. I love Micah, and I want what's best for him. I want him to be happy, even if that means I have to let him go. Sometimes being in love isn't always about getting what you want. Sometimes it's about making sure the other person is happy, even if it means giving up the one person you love the most."

Chapter 19

"See, guys? I *knew* this would eventually happen!" Spence said happily as the four members of *Tempered Souls* sat around his living room table, reading over their new contract. "Anything can happen when you work hard and just keep pushing forward."

He looked up, smiling at everyone as Nik and Zachery clinked their glasses of beer together in a jubilant toast. He looked over at Micah, trying not to wince as he saw how pinched and drawn his face looked. He just knew this news would snap him out of the foul mood he had been in for well over two months now.

"This is what we've been working so hard for, Micah," he said, giving his drummer a huge grin. "Cheer up! We are about to sign a three record deal with the largest recording label in the country. This time next month the five of us will be sipping cocktails on the beaches of LA and this cold, wet state will just be a distant memory in our review mirrors." He slapped his hand on Micah's back, wishing his drummer would start acting normal again.

Micah glanced over to where Spence's girlfriend was curled up on the couch, browsing through her social media feeds. "Must be nice," he muttered.

Micah's Ember

"What?" Spence asked, not quite understanding what his friend had said.

"I said, it must be nice. To have your girlfriend moving with you? Yeah, must be really fucking nice. Unfortunately the one woman I wanted in my life is back in Louisiana and has stopped talking to me, thanks for asking."

Spence rolled his eyes. "You're not about to start that shit again, are you?" He shook his head, resisting the urge to slam his glass of beer down on the table. "Micah, we've been through this. *She* broke up with *you,* remember? And she did you a favor. She's old enough to be your mom, for Christ's sake. We are all about to have our dreams come true and the last thing you or this band needs is bad publicity fresh out of the gate. I mean, fuck, can you just imagine what the media would say? They'd eat you two alive."

Micah sat there staring at Spence. "Is that really all you fucking cared about, was her *age*? You are more worried about how the fans or the industry might react if they knew my girlfriend was older than me than you are about how I feel, how hard this shit has been on me?"

"Oh, so now she's your girlfriend?" Spence asked, interrupting.

Micah stood up, slamming his beer down onto the table. "Hell fucking yes, Spence. Ember was my girlfriend, okay? And now, thanks to you, she probably thinks all she ever was to me was a piece of ass to keep me entertained during the months we weren't on tour."

"Isn't that what she was, Micah? Just something to keep you entertained?" Spence yelled back, returning Micah's glare.

"No, you fucking twat waffle. I love her," he said before he even realized the words were coming

Micah's Ember

from his mouth. He stood perfectly still for a second, the realization hitting him hard.

He picked up his glass and threw it against the wall, watching it shatter. "I love her, Spence, don't you get it? Thanks to you and your fear of how others might view our relationship, I may have lost the one person in my life who I know without a doubt would stand by me every step of the way during the wild ride we are about to embark on."

He sighed. "Do you really think a girl my age would allow me to hang with my female fans, let them kiss me, hug me, flirt with me without going postal every time she witnessed it? But Ember, she sat back with a smile on her face and was proud of what I had accomplished because she knew my heart belonged to her. And at the end of the day, that was enough for us, to know we had each other's back no matter what."

"But now," Micah said as he shook his head, "now I've probably lost the one woman in my life who I not only love with every fiber in my being, but the only woman who could probably handle me being on tour and not be a rabid, jealous bitch ready to rip me a new asshole every time I walked in the door."

The rest of the band sat silent as Micah slowly moved away from the table, the tears stinging the back of his eyes as he finally admitted to what he had been feeling since he first starting talking to her. Somewhere between the lustful nights of cyber-sex and the hours spent chatting about their lives, he had fallen hopeless, head-over-heels in love with a tiny little strawberry blonde with big blue eyes and a Louisiana drawl.

Micah sighed again, feeling the all-too familiar dizziness wash over him as he stumbled, his legs giving out beneath him as the darkness rose up to consume him.

Micah's Ember

Chapter 20

Ember stared at the text message on her phone, her heart hammering so hard inside of her chest she could hear the blood rushing through her veins. The lump inside her throat was threatening to suffocate her where she sat. It took her three times to read through the text completely, alternating between wracking sobs and an overwhelming sense of panic.

Ember, it's Spence. I wanted to apologize for everything I said to you. I was so concerned about the band's image I never stopped to think that I might be hurting Micah. I only want what's best for him. I wanted to let you know he's in the hospital in Detroit. He collapsed yesterday and was admitted early this morning. The doctors aren't really sure what's wrong and are running tests. You may not care, but I thought you should know.

She sat briefly staring at the text before moving suddenly, bolting off her bed. She didn't even stop to think, never once questioned if she was doing the right thing. Micah was sick and no one knew what was wrong. There was only one thing she could do, and she didn't care if anyone else thought it was right or not.

Within an hour she had called into work and was driving to the nearest airport, a plane ticket for the first flight out to Detroit waiting on her, a small

Micah's Ember

suitcase zooming along behind her as she rushed to catch her plane.

Whether it was the right choice or not, it was the only choice which made sense to her. Regardless of what Spence or anyone else thought, she loved Micah, and she was not about to let him go through any of this alone. Whether he loved her or just thought of her as a cyber fling no longer mattered. All she cared about was making sure he was going to be okay.

Micah's Ember

Chapter 21

Her heart was beating so hard inside her chest she feared it would break her ribs. She felt lightheaded, the pounding inside her ears so loud she could scarcely hear her own voice.

"Excuse me," she said, swallowing the lump inside her throat. "I'm looking for Micah Vaughn. Can you tell me what room he is in please?"

She tried to smile, but she honestly felt like she was going to hit the floor.

The lady behind the desk glanced up at her before she typed something into the computer. She smiled at Ember. "Room 604. That's going to be on the sixth floor. Take the elevators there," she said as she nodded toward a set of doors to her right, "and when you get to the sixth floor go straight until you come to the nurse's station. They will be able to give you further directions to his room."

Ember thanked the woman and walked quickly to the elevator, waiting impatiently for the doors to open. She tried not to think about what she was doing as the elevators carried her swiftly to the sixth floor.

She dared not think about what could happen once she saw Micah. Would he be pissed she showed up out of the blue, would he be better now, or worse? She tried not to wonder if he would be happy to see her or if he would demand she leave.

Micah's Ember

She could only hope for the former and try not to think about the latter. Regardless of the outcome, she had to at least try to repair some of the damage she had caused, even if it still meant he didn't want her in his life.

In less than two minutes she was walking down the hall, repeating the directions she had been given at the nurse's station in an attempt to keep her mind from running over all the different scenarios which could play out in the next few minutes. She didn't want to think about what Micah could say to her, didn't want to think about all the possibilities in which he could totally break her heart for good. She had to be prepared to hear him tell her he didn't have any feelings for her and didn't want her in his life, as hard as that may be to hear.

Even if he never wanted to see her again, she had to at least make sure he was okay. She couldn't leave things the way they had been. She knew she should have called him long before now, but as usual, she had been selfish, trying to spare herself more pain even as she tried to convince herself she was really doing it for Micah.

If he didn't want to see her then she could accept that. She felt she at least owed him an explanation, had to let him know she loved him even if he did not feel the same way about her. She shouldn't have just left things the way they had ended during the tour. It was unfair to him to not let him make his own decisions, even if he came to the same conclusion she had.

As Ember rounded the corner, she almost collided with Spence. Startled, she let out a little squeak, causing Nik and Zachery, who were standing a few feet away, to turn around and stare at her.

Micah's Ember

"Ember?" Spence asked, obviously surprised to see her standing in the hallway of a hospital more than a thousand miles from her home.

"Hey, Spence," she said, giving him a timid smile. "I'm sorry, I should have called first, but honestly I didn't even think after I got your text. I hopped on the first flight out, came straight here. How's Micah? Is he going to be okay?"

Spence stood still for a second staring at her in disbelief. Had he really been that wrong about her, about her and Micah's relationship? Why else would she jump on a plane without any thought or real plans, not even knowing if Micah would want to speak to her, and show up just to find out how he was doing?

Spence closed the few feet between them, wrapping his arms around her in an awkward hug. She stood perfectly still, not really sure how to react. "Umm, you okay?" she finally asked.

He let out a short laugh as he released her, shoving his hands into his pockets and giving her a sheepish grin. "I'm sorry, Ember, about everything. I shouldn't have gotten in between you and Micah. I was just trying to protect my friend and in doing so I made things so much worse. For what it's worth, I really am sorry for everything I said. It wasn't fair and I hope you can forgive me some day."

He ducked his head, staring at his feet. "I suck at apologies."

Ember's blue eyes glittered with unshed tears. She smiled, nodding her head. "It's okay, Spence. You said what you did for the same reason why I left when I did, because we both want what's best for him. Neither of us want to see his career flushed down the toilet, not after all the hard work he's put into over the years. But it's not our place to make those decisions for him. I didn't see that

Micah's Ember

before, and I just hope he can forgive me for not letting him make his own decisions about us." She paused, looking over at the closed hospital door. "Have the doctor's said anything about what's wrong?"

"They say it's stress. He hasn't been eating well and he already had a heart murmur. The combination of fatigue, inadequate diet, and stress caused some minor heart palpitations. A lot has happened in the past few months. But I think Micah should be the one to tell you."

She looked at him with worry, her small teeth biting her lower lip. "Does he know I'm here?" she asked before rolling her eyes. "Ugh, of course he doesn't know I'm here."

Spence shook his head, laughing. "No. You never texted me back so I just assumed you weren't interested in what was going on." He ducked his head in embarrassment. "I guess I should have known you would pull something like this."

She smiled, but it was a bitter-sweet smile. "Do you think he wants to see me? I mean, if he's already stressed out, I'm afraid my presence could make things worse, you know? I don't want to cause him any more pain," she said as her eyes darted around the small hallway. "Spence, you're his friend. You've been around him these past few months since I left like I did. Should I even go in there?"

Spence smiled. "Let me go in first, see how he's feeling, okay?"

She nodded, feeling her heart skip a beat as she watched Spence disappear inside of Micah's room. The entire rest of her life hinged on what was about to be said inside that small room. All she could do now was wait to see if she could

Micah's Ember

finally start breathing again, or if her heart was going to be crushed once and for all.

***

Spence closed the door behind him quietly, walking over to the hospital bed. Micah lay on his back, his eyes staring up at the ceiling as the heart monitor beeped steadily in the background.

"Hey, Micah, how are you?"

His drummer slowly turned his head, but his eyes stared right through his friend. "Fine," he mumbled before he turned his head slowly back to once again stare at the ceiling. "When are they letting me out of here?"

"Probably tomorrow. They just want to make sure all your tests results are normal and monitor you for another twenty-four hours." He sat down in the tiny chair by the bed only to stand right back up again. "You've got to get well, you know? We've got so much to do in the next few weeks with moving and getting our contracts in and all."

Micah continued to stare at the ceiling. "Uh huh, I know. I'll be out of here tomorrow and we can get everything signed, start getting packed," he said in a monotone, his voice sounding flat and dead.

Spence sighed. This wasn't going to be easy, and he didn't like the thought of upsetting Micah further, but at least he was in the right place if he was going to have another episode. "Listen, Micah, I owe you an apology."

The heart monitor let out a small series of chirps before settling back into a normal pattern. Micah's dull aquamarine eyes darted over to his vocalist, but he didn't say anything. He watched as Spence shoved his hand through his hair, causing it to stand on end.

Micah's Ember

"I'm sorry, about everything I said about you and Ember. You were right, it was none of my business. I was only trying to protect you, this band, and all the hard work we've put into everything these past few years. But I think I made things worse, and I'm sorry."

Micah stared at him for a second before he nodded and then went back to staring at the ceiling. "Doesn't matter, Spence. You may have been right. She hasn't bothered to call or text or reach out to me in any way since she left. I was stupid to think Em could be happy with some punk-ass kid in a rock band. She's better off with some corporate suit driving a beamer or something."

Spence moved toward the door, saying, "Yeah, I wouldn't be so sure about that."

"What are you talking about?"

"Well, there's someone here to see you," Spence said.

Micah glanced at his friend before he grunted. "Please tell me you didn't call my mom."

Spence chuckled. "No, I didn't even think about calling your mom to be honest," he said before he opened the door, motioning for someone to come into the room.

Micah saw movement out of the corner of his eye, but kept staring at the ceiling, not really caring who was there.

Ember walked slowly toward the bed, her heart thudding heavily in her chest as she saw the man she loved more than anything else in this world laying still and pale in the bed.

She wished Spence had warned her about what she was walking in to. She knew she had had a hard time in the past few months and had lost considerable weight, but it appeared Micah hadn't fared much better. He looked like he had lost

Micah's Ember

nearly thirty pounds, his face drawn and pinched, his skin about as sallow-looking as hers.

"Micah?" His name was barely a whisper on his lips, but it was enough.

He turned his head slowly, the heart monitor beeping erratically as his heart suddenly began racing at the sight of her. He blinked, wondering if he was dreaming.

But how could he be dreaming? She was still just as beautiful as he remembered, but like him, their time apart had not been kind to her. She was thinner, paler, her usual strawberry blonde locks dull.

"Ember?" he asked hoarsely as he tried to sit up in the bed.

Time suddenly slowed for her as she stood in the middle of the room, staring at the man who had somehow managed to win over her heart in such a short amount of time. Nothing mattered at that moment. She didn't care if he never wanted to see her again. Somehow it didn't matter if he told her to leave and never come back. What was most important to her at that very moment was seeing him safe, even if she could possibly be seeing him for the last time.

She couldn't stop the tears from flowing down her cheeks as she rushed to him, throwing herself into his arms as she sobbed. He looked so pale, his eyes sunken just as hers was.

"I'm sorry, Micah. I'll leave if you want me to, but I had to make sure you were going to be okay," she said, pulling back to plant small, delicate kisses all over his face. "I shouldn't have left things like I did. I should have called, should have explained, should have done anything but just cut you out of my life. I thought I was doing what was best for you."

Micah's Ember

She stopped abruptly, pulling back so she could see him, her hands still on his face as she smiled through her tears. "I know it's crazy and other people aren't going to understand it. I know people are going to talk and you are going to get a lot of shit because of it. But," she said, taking a deep breath, "somewhere in the past seven months I fell head-over-heels in love with you, Micah. I don't expect you to love me back, but I couldn't leave things the way they were between us and not let you know how I truly feel. It's not fair of me to expect you to want to date someone so much older than you, but I felt you at least deserved to know the truth."

She continued, "I left that day because I knew people wouldn't be able to see past our age difference. I was afraid you were going to sabotage all the hard work you had put into making a name for yourself, and I just couldn't let you do that, not for someone who could very well bring down the whole band. I'll understand if you never want to see me again, never want to talk to me again. If you want me to leave, I will. I just wanted you to know I didn't want things to end between us the way they did, and I'm sorry."

Micah's head was reeling with so many thoughts and emotions, but none of it mattered. The last two months being away from her didn't matter, all the angry words between him and Spence didn't matter. Not even the contract he was about to sign really mattered because if she wasn't in his life, then all of his dreams weren't really coming true. As much as he had worked toward the day when he could finally sign a huge recording contract, as wonderful as he thought it would all be once that day finally arrived, it paled in comparison to what was happening right now. All that mattered, the only thing he really truly

Micah's Ember

wanted out of life was her, and she was here now. And she loved him.

He pulled her close, his eyes staring into hers before he pulled her down and kissed her tenderly, his lips soft and warm. She melted into him, her arms wrapping around his neck as her heart swelled with more happiness and love than she had ever felt before.

"I love you, Ember," he said as he held her close, his forehead pressed against hers. "I don't care what everyone else things, I don't care how much they talk. All that matter is we are comfortable with how things are between us. I want you by my side, sharing in this crazy ride wherever it may take us. I can't imagine my life without you in it, and I don't want to be away from you for even one more minute. I know it's not fair of me to ask, but would you consider moving to be with me?"

The tears slid down her face as she nodded her head, kissing him again. "You mean it? You really want me to move up here to be with you?"

"Um, actually, I'm asking you to move with me to California. We just got offered a three record deal with the largest label in the country. We're moving to Los Angeles in three weeks," he said with a laugh as he tenderly wiped the tears from her cheeks, a soft smile on his lips as he searched her face.

She grinned at him. "So you want me to move to California with you?"

He nodded, picking up her hand and kissing the palm.

She sighed, loving how his lips felt on her body. "I'm glad, because earlier today I told my boss I was moving."

He stared at her, his eyes searching hers. "You quit your job just to move up here?"

Micah's Ember

"Not exactly. That place would fall apart without me. They agreed to let me work from home, wherever that may be. Here, California, even Hell if need be. I'd follow you to the ends of the earth, all you have to do is ask."

He pulled her close, holding her tightly. "I love you, Micah," she said. "No matter where you go, no matter what you do, I'll always be by your side. My home is wherever you are, and I never want to be apart from you again.

Micah's Ember

Epilogue

"I told you we'd all be sitting around sipping cocktails on the beach by now," Spence said as he held up his martini glass.

His girlfriend Renee and his band mates, Zachery and Nik, held up their glasses as they all cheered, taking a swallow of their drinks.

Micah stared out over the water, smiling as a small hand reached around to hold out a fresh bottle of beer. He turned, taking the bottle and setting it on the table beside him.

"Did you ever see such a beautiful sight?" a soft voice asked.

"Yes, every time I look at you," he whispered, pulling her down into his lap.

"Is this everything you thought it would be?" she asked as the wind blew her strawberry blonde hair around her face.

He reached up to tuck a wayward strand behind Ember's ear, smiling as he did so. "Yes," he said as he wrapped his arms around her, loving the way she pressed her body against his. "It's everything I ever dreamed it would be, and so much more."

She giggled as she leaned in to kiss him, gasping as his hand grabbed her ass. "Hey, no fair teasing if you aren't planning on pleasing," she said.

Micah's Ember

"Ah, who said I didn't plan on pleasing? I've got to keep my Mistress happy, right?" he asked.

"Ugh, you two go get a room," Spence said, grinning at the two of them where they sat cuddled together a few feet away.

Micah flipped him off, pulling Ember closer.

She giggled again, wrapping her fingers through his. He held up his arm, nodding toward the leather bracelet he wore. "Damn right you do," she said as she smiled, the sunlight glinting off the metal plate on the front of the bracelet. For a fraction of a second the delicate inscription was obscured by the reflection of the sun, her mind unconsciously remembering the words written there ...

Owned by Mistress – Live without fear, love without limits. Yours always, Ember.

The End

Micah's Ember

A Word from the Author

I have to say a very special thanks to Micah J. Link, the drummer for A War Within, who was so gracious when I informed him he was my muse for this book. As many of my readers know, I had always dreamed of studying music journalism in college, but somewhere between graduation, marriage, and three children, my dreams of working for a large magazine interviewing my favorite bands somehow morphed into a business degree which came much later in life. As much as I love reading and creating my fictional worlds, my first love will always be music. Because of this, I do all I can to help spread the word on all the wonderful bands I have been so fortunate to discover over the past few years.

Many of these bands have been the driving force behind the spark of my imagination, and Micah has been no exception. Because of him, A War Within, and their commitment to each other, the band, and their careers, *Micah's Ember* was born. To Micah, Spencer, Nikhil, and Zach, you guys rock. I wish you nothing but success and happiness wherever your lives and careers may take you.

Spencer, please don't hate me for making you into the "bad" guy. You are still cool as fuck to me.

Micah, thank you again for being such a cool and wonderful person. You are truly something special and I hope you find all the happiness in life that you deserve.

XOXO
Nicola

Micah's Ember

About the Author

Nicola C. Matthews was born in September 1975 in Biloxi, MS. Raised in southern Mississippi, she still resides in her small hometown with her husband of over twenty years, their three children, and their pet Yorkie, Lily-Claire. She loves music and her favorite thing to do to de-stress is crank up the tunes and hit the treadmill. Nicola enjoys reading as well as watching movies, shopping, and meeting new people. Her favorite genres include mystery thrillers and supernatural/fantasy movies and books.

Nicola's love affair with reading and books first began at the age of seven, when she immolated her favorite author at the time, Dr. Seuss. As the years passed, her passion for writing and reading turned into a way to escape a broken and oftentimes violent home life. She funneled her love for all things creative into her writing, penning her first novel at the age of thirteen.

Throughout high school, Nikki would continue to pen two additional novels and a host of short stories and poems. At the age of fifteen, she began her journey into the publishing industry, spending her weekends at the local library researching the

Micah's Ember

industry, writing query letters, and sending out sample chapters to publishers.

By her graduating year, Nicola had racked up several hundred rejection letters from every publisher she could find. Undaunted, she continued to write over the years, but raising a growing family took precedent over her fledgling career. In 2006, at the urging of a large social media audience through her Yahoo!360 page, she began to research self-publishing. In 2009, her first novel *Temptation* was published under her own publishing house. After taking a break to finish her business degree, Nicola continued to write and publish under her house name.

Vindictus, The Dark Lord published in December 2010.

Various shorts, including bestsellers "The Devil's Slave" and "Master" published periodically from 2011 – 2013.

The Red Fang, the first book in the BEFORE THE SUN RISES SERIES, published in June 2011, and would be relaunched through the BOOKTROPE EDITIONS brand in August 2015. After the publisher closed its doors in May of 2016, the book was relaunched through X-Cite Press, an imprint of X-Isle United Publishers.

Immortal Sins, the second book in the BEFORE THE SUN RISES SERIES published in 2014.

Nicola would team up with a fellow erotica writer and release a new romantic comedy series, SWEET SEDUCTIONS. The first two books in the series, *The Taming of Andy Savage* and *Collaring Ash* were released in November 2015 and February 2016 respectively.

Nicola's latest creation, a romantic paranormal thriller entitled *Hell's Ballad* released in May 2016.

Today, Nicola works full time for a multi-million-dollar technology reseller and continues to

Micah's Ember

write and publish under her house name. Her lifelong dream, aside from one day becoming a NYT Best Selling Author, is to help other writers realize their dream of becoming published authors.

In addition to owning X-Isle United Publishers, the publishing house she founded in 2008, she has since added two imprints to the publishing house, X-Cite Press and X-Treme books. In 2014, she launched a small marketing firm in conjunction with the publishing house, X-Isle Promotions. Nicola also owns and operates a small graphic art company as well.

Micah's Ember

Connect with the Author

Nicola on the Web
http://NicolaCMatthews.com

Follow Nicola on Twitter
@ncmatthews

Join Nicola on Facebook
http://facebook.com/groups/nikkisbookdivas
http://facebook.com/nicolacmatthews

Follow Nicola on Instagram
@NicolaCMatthews

Follow Nicola on Amazon
http://amazon.com/author/nicolamatthews

Enjoyed this tale? Please be sure to leave a review at your favorite retailer outlet. Reviews are the easiest and best way to show your support for your favorite authors and books!

Micah's Ember

The Taming of Andy Savage

Sweet Seductions Series

Book 1

By Nicola C. Matthews & Angel H. Scott

Nicolette pushed her way through the crowd, the tightly packed bodies writhing in time to the pounding chords ripping from Jacob's guitar. Everyone around her was screaming, but the sound could not be heard through the driving beat engulfing them all like a living, breathing thing. Andy's voice rose above the music, deep, perfect, the sound sending many of the women in the room into a lust-filled swoon.

As the last chords of music waned, a young woman screamed out, "*I love you, Andy!*"

From somewhere within the darkness of the stage, a dark voice answered. "I love you, too," he said as the overhead lights suddenly flashed rapidly. Everyone in the crowd screamed as Andy stood to the side of the stage with a huge grin on his face. He dipped his head forward and then whipped it back, tossing his shoulder-length black hair back out of his face.

Nicolette felt a shuddering tingle race up her spine and then settle between her legs. She had to

Micah's Ember

fight the urge to rush the stage and shove her tongue down his throat and her hands down his pants. He was the epitome of every rock star cliché all rolled into one. He was tall and had so many tattoos on his arms it was hard to tell where one ended and the other began. He had enough piercings to make a Voodoo doll jealous, and he oozed more sex appeal than any man had the right to, alive or undead. His voice was deep, dark, and melodic. She wasn't sure which she found more attractive, his voice, his beautiful smile, or his quick wit and sense of humor. He was, for lack of a better word, absolutely *perfect.*

White Coffin had been on the stage for nearly an hour, their set almost complete. Nicolette held onto her position to the left of the stage, wrapping her hands around the barricade. It was the only thing keeping the patrons of THE FANGGASM nightclub from rushing the stage, and from the five vampires who currently occupied it. In just three more songs the band would be through for the night, and Nicolette's job would just be beginning.

Nicolette Vampskin was the leading field journalist for *The Alternative Underground*, the single most popular vampire metal magazine and blog in the industry. She had landed the job fresh out of high school. *The Underground* had been a fledgling magazine at the time. It was the very first publication which not only sought out supernatural musicians, but actively sent out human reporters to interview the bands. Within a year she had become the magazine's lead reporter, and in the process she also became the biggest fang-whore in the entire country.

As the band prepared for their final encore, she moved toward the back of the stage, flashing her PRESS badge at one of the guards keeping all the groupies at bay. There was absolutely no need to do this; she was at the club every weekend and every security guard and bouncer in the building knew her by name. But, to be honest, she thoroughly enjoyed the nasty looks all the skank-whores gave her. It gave her a perverse sense of pleasure knowing she was about to sit in the company of the best damn metal band the world had ever known, while they were all resigned to hold up "I WANNA FUCK YOU ASH!" signs in hopes the bassist might look their way. She almost felt sorry for them. But then again, she hadn't exactly made a name for herself by feeling sorry for people.

She rounded the side of the stage just as the band thanked everyone for coming out, the five of them moving so quickly down the stairs they all nearly collided into each other as Andy Savage stopped suddenly on the last step. His blue eyes locked onto her as she planted herself squarely in front of him. Those intense baby blues raked over her, taking in her ripped leggings, short skirt, shredded White Coffin tee, and the rounded mounds the shirt barely concealed.

"Nicolette Vampskin," she said as she held out her hand.

Andy paused, much longer than was necessary for a vampire, giving his actions a very human feel.

He took her hand and shook it lightly. "I know who you are, Ms. Vampskin. When they told me we were being interviewed for *The Underground*, I never in my wildest dreams thought they would be sending you."

She laughed, tossing her head back, exposing the length of her neck for a moment. The various white scars from multiple vampire bites were clearly visible on her pale skin.

Andy moved suddenly, his body quickly closing the few inches separating them. Startled,

Micah's Ember

Nicolette froze as his hand moved to cradle the back of her neck. He gently moved her head to the side as he brushed a few loose auburn tendrils of hair from her neck, his eyes looking over the scars. He let go of her just as quickly as he had grabbed hold of her.

"You do get around, don't you?" he asked, not really expecting an answer. He turned his head, nodding slightly. The other four members jumped off the steps, walking casually toward one of the back exits.

"I see my reputation precedes me," she muttered.

"Yes, it does, but I understand the fascination," he said as he ducked his head closer to hers. "How do you think I ended up this way?" he whispered, tilting his own head to the side. She caught a quick glimpse of the line of tiny, white scars marring the side of his neck, scars that greatly resembled her own vampire track marks.

She smiled in amusement. Obviously she wasn't the only one who had a vampire fetish. "I assure you, Andy, I am just here on business," she replied, even though she knew it wasn't entirely true.

"When are you going to learn to share?" Ash Pardue asked as he turned around, walking backward as he gave Andy a large, fangy grin. He eyed Nicolette openly, causing her to squirm just a bit. She wasn't sure how they had managed to cram so many hot vampires into one band, but there they all were, looking like a vision straight from a groupie's wet dream.

"Next time, man," Andy replied as his eyes moved back to Nicolette. "Promise."

Micah's Ember

Hells Ballad

By Nicola C. Matthews

It was the dream again, that same damn dream, the one which left his heart pounding mercilessly in his chest every time he awoke from it. He was standing over Eva, the woman he loved more than life itself, the knife in his hand glinting evilly from the dancing flames of the fire as he prepared to carry out the ritual.

The look in her aquamarine-colored eyes was one of terror beyond measure as she struggled to free herself from the ropes. She begged him to stop, crying desperately as she whispered how much she loved him, begging to know why he was doing this.

"Jaxon, please! You have been hallucinating again. You haven't been sleeping and it's playing tricks on your mind. Please don't hurt us!"

"You know I have to do this, Eva. You know it can't be allowed to live. It will destroy us all!"

The woman he loved shook her head fiercely as the tears rolled down her face. She was shaking in terror, her eyes huge in her pretty face. "There's nothing wrong with our baby, Jax! You're not well. You just need some sleep," she whispered, her voice catching in her throat. "Please, please don't do this."

"I have to," he whispered.

"No, you don't. I know you don't really want to hurt us, Jax. I know you love us, I know you love me and our baby. Please, Jaxon, please untie me and let's get you to the hospital before it's too late."

Micah's Ember

"It's not too late, Eva, not if I kill it now. Please be still. I don't want this to hurt any more than it has to."

"Jaxon, please, no!"

For a moment the dream shifted, and Eva was no longer strapped to the altar, but instead was standing right behind him, begging him to understand why she was breaking up with him. She had been cutting up potatoes, her hand brandishing the knife as she grew more and more agitated. At some point he had taken the knife from her, worried she might hurt herself or him. It was only a flicker, a slight shifting in the scene, and she was once again tied down, begging for her life.

He lifted the knife above his head and plunged it deep into her body, cutting off her pleas of mercy as the blade sliced through her abdomen effortlessly, allowing him easy access to the still squirming form writhing inside of her. "We'll be safe now, Eva, and we can be together, forever, just the way we always wanted."

In that one fatal blow he had sealed his deal with the Dark Prince, forever binding his life and soul to the evil one.

Jax Monroe jerked awake, his entire body shaking, his skin drenched in sweat. His dark brown eyes darted around the tiny coffin-like compartment, taking in his surroundings as the entire floor beneath him lurched slightly. He sat up as a tiny knock came to the collapsible door which separated the sleeping area from the rest of the bus.

"Jax, we're about half an hour out from the venue," Rave said through the closed door. "You up?"

Jax ran his hand through his damp hair, mumbling, "Yeah, okay, I'm up."

Micah's Ember

He rolled out of the small bunk as the tour bus lurched forward once again, finally settling into a rhythm which could barely be felt as they continued on their journey. Jax moved to the tiny bath in the corner, splashing water onto his face. He looked at himself, the devil in the mirror staring back, but he didn't see his own reflection. He was lost deep in thought, his mind replaying the dream over and over again. The two different dreamscapes and the reality of what had really happened were all so jumbled up inside his head.

He thought back to that night so many years ago, remembering the scene as if it had happened only yesterday. The woman tied to the altar had not been Eva, his high school sweetheart. She had left him several years prior to that night, right before he dropped out of high school. She had told him she couldn't be with anyone who wasn't going to make something of himself one day. His dreams of becoming a rock legend were not good enough for her, or so she had said. She had left him a few days later, moving out of state with his best friend at the time, the best friend who had been accepted into medical school.

He had eventually found his way in the world, although it had been far from easy. He had moved to Los Angeles a few months shy of his eighteenth birthday with nothing more than a broken down delivery van, a few clothes, and barely a hundred dollars to his name. He had spent the next three years doing odd jobs and anything else which fell into his lap to keep food in his stomach and strings on his guitar.

Those first few years had been hell on earth for him. It was difficult to keep a job while living out of the back of his van, the only access he had to running water being a 'sink shower' taken at various convenience stores whenever he got the

Micah's Ember

chance. He was almost always hungry and agents were constantly telling him he wasn't going to make it in the industry. They didn't want metal groups with wild hair and black eyeliner, they wanted cute boy bands who were just as good at sucking cock as they were at turning their fan girls into screaming piles of mush. He was determined if nothing else, and just when he thought he was either going to die or have to return to his bastard of a father, he got mixed up with people who could help him see his dreams come true, and he never looked back.

Even now as the events of that long-ago night replayed through his subconscious on an endless loop, he did not regret his decision. As the dreams interfered more and more with his sleep, causing him to feel tired and listless most days, the endless nights of sleeplessness fading together into a sea of faceless fans all screaming his name, he still did not regret one moment since that night. If anything, he wished he would have bargained for more time.

"Jax, man, we're almost there," Rave said as he opened the door just a crack to peer in, his grey-blue eyes smudged with a thick ring of black eyeliner.

Jax's brown eyes shifted over to look at his band mate in the mirror. Rave was freshly shaved, his eyeliner looking like he had slept in it for days instead of being freshly applied, something Jax had yet to master. The natural dark brown hair he had been born with was dyed a perfect shade of Raven Black, his signature color which was only part of the reason why he took on the stage name when the band came together.

"You want to head straight there or stop off at the hotel first?"

Micah's Ember

Jax stifled a yawn with the back of his hand before answering. "Let's just go straight there and get set up, get at least one sound check in before we head over to the hotel."

Rave nodded his head. "Sure thing, I'll let Wheels know he-"

Rave stopped mid-sentence as a loud scream came from the front of the bus. "You fucking son-of-a-bitch, how many times have I told you to not fucking do that shit!"

Rave moved out of the way as Jax hurried out of the small compartment which housed the bands' bunks and small bath. He almost collided with Treble and Tribe as the two of them wrestled in the narrow hallway in the middle in the bus.

"What the hell are you two doing?" Jax asked, watching as his other guitarist and drummer bumped along the walls in their tussle.

The two of them stopped, Treble holding Tribe in a headlock, the white of Treble's hair mixing in with the black onyx locks of Tribe's waist-length hair. They looked at Jax like he was some deranged lunatic who had suddenly materialized in the middle of their home.

"Dude," Treble said, looking Jax up and down in disbelief. "What the hell did you do after last night's show?"

Micah's Ember

The Red Fang

Before the Sun Rises Series
Book 1
By Nicola C. Matthews

Ashton Jones was a serial killer. Until he was recruited by the Shield of Humanity organization, he had only had the pleasure of torturing humans. Now he'd been given the very unique opportunity to not only torture, but possibly even kill a vampire. He was finding the entire experience very much to his liking.

The young female vampire strapped to the table only looked young. At least, she *used* to look young. The vampire known as Jasmine had been starved of blood for nearly a month now. Had she not been feeding on a regular basis, Ashton's systematic starvation of the vampire would not have worked. However, although she might have been nearing eighty years a vampire, she was still feeding off the blood of the living nearly every day.

The starvation had made the vampire weaker both physically and mentally, but it also made her very dangerous. Since her body was used to receiving fresh blood on a regular basis, the bloodlust had taken hold of her mind about two weeks into Ashton's *session* with her.

Starvation was a great tool to use when interrogating a vampire, but one had to be careful. Ashton had been forced to crank up his torture a few notches in order to drag her mind back from the frenzy it was staying in, due to the starvation

Micah's Ember

tactic. The female's bones had been broken so many times they were no longer healing properly, thanks in part to the lack of fresh blood, and also simply because they *had* been broken so many times. The consistent breaking in the same place so many dozens of times had now produced unsightly lumps and bulges all over the vampire's arms and legs.

This information in itself was useful to the agency, especially since Ashton had been hired specifically to extract as much information out of the vampire as possible. The agency had already conducted numerous experiments on the vampire and werewolf anatomy. What they wanted now was the information their experimentation could not tell them.

Jasmine's sunken brown eyes followed Ashton as he moved toward the table that held the small bag of human blood. She tried to lick her cracked lips, but her mouth had stopped producing saliva a few days ago. The only thing that gave her any relief now were the few teaspoons of blood Ashton gave her from time to time, either as a reward for giving him the information he wanted or as a way to keep the bloodlust from taking over her mind so completely.

"Please, Ashton, I'm begging you. End it! I've told you everything I know. Please ... *Please* ... kill me already. I simply cannot bear it any longer!"

Ashton smiled, although with his back turned to the undead creature, she couldn't see the cruelty stamped on his handsome face.

"I have no intentions of killing you, Jasmine," he said quietly.

The vampire let out a high pitched wail. "What more do you want from me?" she screamed, thrashing around on the table in another attempt to get loose of the restraints. "I don't know

Micah's Ember

anything more than what I have already said to you hundreds of times now!"

She began crying again, the sobs almost painful to Ashton's ears. The agency thought the sound was some type of warning system the vampires could use to alert each other of danger. It was also a weapon of sorts, as the high-pitched frequency could really hurt the human ear if it was used right.

Now the vampire was crying uncontrollably, babbling almost incoherently in between the racking sobs. "The werewolves don't carry viruses. The scientists have already told the world this. They don't become werewolves or any other type of wereanimal by being bitten. That's a bunch of nonsense invented for the movies." She continued to pull at the metal restraints, her frightened, tear-filled eyes darting around the room as she talked.

"It's like the scientists say, it's a gene some of them carry that gets switched on at some point in their lives. I don't know how it works. I just know once the gene is activated the person is no longer susceptible to any type of disease."

Ashton turned away from the small table where he had been busy, loving how Jasmine's eyes grew wide in terror as she saw the bone saw he carried in his hand.

"The human scientists already know everything I know about werewolves, and you people know more than the scientists do!"

Ashton pushed the button on the bone saw a few times, the high-pitched buzz filling the room. Jasmine cringed at the sound and began whimpering, her body thrashing on the table in spasms driven by fear.

"What about the vampires?" he asked.

She shook her head violently. "I already told you!" she screamed.

Micah's Ember

Ashton turned on the saw again. Jasmine began rattling off the same information she had already told him a dozen times before in the past few months. "You don't become a vampire by being bitten, either! We don't know it works."

The small female vampire pulled her arms against the restraints, the metal digging so deep into her flesh the bones were close to breaking. She was so desperate to escape she was causing almost as much damage to her body as Ashton had. *Almost*.

"If it's not a virus, then how do you go about making new vampires?" he asked, playing with the button on the saw.

The vampire hissed at the sound, but she kept talking. "Whoever is being embraced must be drained of blood. They have to be nearly dead for the transformation to work. Once the human is almost dead, you have to feed them the sire's blood." She kept pulling at the restraints, the bones beginning to fracture under the strain. The vampire did not seem to notice. "But they have to be almost dead! If they are not nearing death then it won't work."

"Tell me more about the blood, Jasmine," he whispered softly, reaching down to grasp her right arm in his hand. He yanked the arm upward suddenly, forcibly, snapping the bone at the wrist.

"Be still, or you'll break the other one," he said quietly.

The vampire's sunken eyes were huge in her pale face, the pupils dilated so much there was barely any white visible in them at all. She only groaned when the bone of her arm broke, her fear so great she could concentrate on little else.

Her breathing was heavy and erratic as she continued to tell Ashton the same things that had now been repeated a hundred times. "I don't know

Micah's Ember

why our blood makes a regular human stronger when they drink it!" She began shaking her head back and forth as Ashton came closer with the saw, flicking the button on and off as the vampire began to shake uncontrollably on the table.

"I don't know who discovered the properties of our blood. I don't know who began selling it as a designer drug. I *don't know,* Ashton, I swear I don't! If I knew I would tell you. My sire abandoned me right after I was embraced. He left me to fend for myself! If I knew of an older vampire who knew these things I would tell you! I swear it, Ashton! *Please don't!*"

Jasmine's screams echoed off the white tiled walls as Ashton turned on the saw and placed it against her naked abdomen.

"Last chance to tell me something useful," he said happily.

"I don't know anything else!" she shrieked.

Ashton only smiled, the sound of the vampire's screams eventually being drowned out by the droning of the saw blade as the bits of flesh and blood spattered his face and hands. God, how he loved his job!

Micah's Ember

Micah's Ember

10325886R00116

Made in the USA
Middletown, DE
12 November 2018